"I've got another job that you can do for the King, an important job. A risky job. He's given me authority to swear you into the Guard without binding you. Are you willing to serve?"

But the rules said . . . Stalwart realized that he was standing there like a lummox with his mouth open. *"Yes, sir!"*

"Are you certain?" Bandit asked quietly. "This is where I need that brave-and-reliable Stalwart. It will be dangerous. A Blade never needs to worry about courage, because his binding makes him brave. Are you stalwart enough, Candidate Stalwart? Can you take on a dangerous job without being bound?"

He hadn't yet said what the job was. Apparently the planning had been going on for months and the King himself had authorized it. It must be important. Stalwart's heart thundered in his throat.

"I'll try my best, sir."

"I can't ask for more. Come with me."

Look for These Avon Eos Books by
Dave Duncan

The King's Blades

THE GILDED CHAIN
LORD OF THE FIRE LANDS

The *Great Games* Trilogy

PAST IMPERATIVE:
ROUND ONE OF THE GREAT GAME

PRESENT TENSE:
ROUND TWO OF THE GREAT GAME

FUTURE INDEFINITE:
ROUND THREE OF THE GREAT GAME

**Visit Dave Duncan's website at
http://www.cadvision.com/daveduncan/**

SIR STALWART

Book One of the King's Daggers

DAVE DUNCAN

AVON BOOKS ◆ NEW YORK

AVON BOOKS, INC.
1350 Avenue of the Americas
New York, New York 10019

Copyright © 1999 by Dave Duncan
Excerpt from *The Gilded Chain: A Tale of the King's Blades* copyright © 1999 by Dave Duncan
Published by arrangement with the author
Library of Congress Catalog Card Number: 99-94643
ISBN: 0-380-80098-5
www.avonbooks.com

First Avon Books Printing: November 1999

AVON BOOKS TRADEMARK REG. U.S. PAT. OFF. AND IN OTHER COUNTRIES, MARCA REGISTRADA, HECHO EN U.S.A.

Printed in the U.S.A.

WCD   10 9 8 7 6 5 4 3 2 1

The Minstrel Boy to the war is gone,
*   In the ranks of death you'll find him;*
His father's sword he has girded on,
*   And his wild harp slung behind him.*

—THOMAS MOORE

Contents

x   Contents

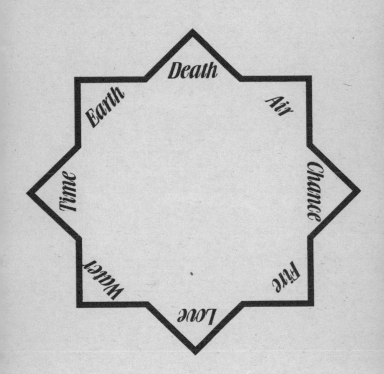

SIR STALWART

Book One of the King's Daggers

Rude Awakening

ABOUT AN HOUR BEFORE DAWN SOME IDIOT BLEW a deafening blast on a bugle right under the dormitory window. Nine boys lurched up out of deep sleep with yells of alarm, then registered the clattering of iron-clad hooves on the cobbles of the courtyard. Nine blankets flew off, eighteen bare feet hit the boards at almost the same instant, nine bodies dived for the window.

Stalwart prided himself on being the fastest man in the senior class, but he was also the smallest. He did reach the window first, only to be hurled aside by a flying wedge of superior muscle. No matter! It was still too dark outside to see much, and he could guess what was happening—the King had come to Ironhall. Judging by the racket, he was being escorted by the entire Royal Guard, a hundred strong.

"When did the King ever travel by night before?" someone cried, probably Rufus.

"Never!" That was Orvil, who was Prime,

1

meaning he had been in Ironhall longer than anyone. "And he used to bring a dozen Blades with him, no more."

Eighteen eyes shone wide in the gloom as the senior class thought about King Ambrose skulking around by night and needing so many bodyguards. Nine naked or near-naked youngsters shivered in the predawn chill. The unheralded royal visit was a chilling reminder of the Monster War. For the last eight months or so—starting with the terrible Night of Dogs—unknown sorcerers had repeatedly tried to kill the King of Chivial, killing many of the Blades in his Guard in the process. The only reason he ever came to Ironhall was to enlist new Blades, who would be chosen from the senior class—the very nine present in that dormitory. How many would he take this time? Tonight at midnight he would strike a sword through their hearts in a magical ritual to bind them to absolute loyalty, companions in the Loyal and Ancient Order of the King's Blades.

How many of them?

"Well, don't all stand there with your tongues hanging out!" yelled Panther. "Get dressed! Your King wants you!"

Eight seniors sprang into motion, quickly followed by Panther himself as he realized he wasn't wearing anything either.

*   *   *

Someone struck a flint. Spark on tinder, flame on candle, many candle flames ... With nervy haste the nine seniors rummaged in hampers to find their best and cleanest—breeches, hose, shirts, doublets, jerkins. Cloaks and boots and hats. Comb hair. Those who needed to shave began doing so—painfully, because no one dared run and fetch hot water lest he be absent when the summons came. There was some angry jostling around the candles and tiny mirrors.

Shaving was not yet one of Stalwart's problems. He sat on the edge of his bed and hugged himself, miserably uncertain whether the knot in his innards was wild excitement or just terror. He *wanted* to be chosen this time! Of course he wanted to be chosen! Why else had he spent the last four years working his heart out here in Ironhall if not to become a Blade? True, he was the youngest of the seniors, but he ranked fifth in seniority, and candidates always left Ironhall in the order in which they had come. He was worthy! Day in and day out he was the best on the fencing ground. And yet ... Until the Night of Dogs a career in the Royal Guard had been a sinecure, easy pickings, ten years of lounging around the court charming beautiful ladies. Now it was as dangerous as lion wrestling. Two dozen members of the Order had died in the last half year. Ironhall was rushing boys through training faster than it had in centuries. None of the current seniors, even Prime, had been in the school for the standard five years.

"There's no great hurry," Orvil said squeakily, although he had been moving as fast as anyone. "First the King talks with Grand Master and tells him how many of us he wants. Then Grand Master sends the Brat to fetch us." Everyone knew this, because he had told them at least a dozen times. He had been present the last time, two months ago. "They always send for one more than they are going to bind, so he can—"

The door flew open. Two shavers cut themselves and screamed in fury. In walked Sir Dreadnought, Deputy Commander of the Guard.

"How many?" everyone yelled in unison.

Dreadnought closed the door and folded his arms. He surveyed the room in the dim light, smiling grimly. "As many of you as Grand Master can bear to part with. I just came to make sure none of you goes sneaking down to the kitchens. A whole day's fasting before a binding, remember."

The discomfort inside Stalwart, which had been worry, instantly became ravening hunger instead. Out in the corridor a mob of chattering, jabbering juniors headed for the stairs—sopranos and beansprouts. The seniors clustered closer around Dreadnought, most of them still soaped for shaving.

"Have there been more attacks on the King?" Orvil asked.

"State secret. I'm not allowed to tell you that until you're bound." Dreadnought was a good man, a superb swordsman. He had won the King's Cup for the second time that summer, which meant he was probably the finest fencer in the entire world at the moment. On his jerkin he sported a four-pointed diamond-studded badge to show he was a member of the White Star, the highest order of chivalry in the country. Very few Blades had ever been admitted to the Star, but he had turned up wearing this wonderful thing two months ago. He'd conceded only that he had won it "killing something," but the other men in the Guard had added blood-curdling details of a shambling half-human monstrosity that had gone after the King when he was out hunting. Its fangs and talons had disposed of two other Blades and a horse before Dreadnought slew it. An excellent man!

A bit lacking in humor, maybe. You could tell a lot about a Blade by the name he gave his sword, and his was called *Honor*. Dull!

"And you *still* don't know who's doing this?" Orvil persisted.

"If the Guard knew that, sonny, blood would be shed and balefires lit. No matter how good their sorcery is."

Stalwart asked, "How many swords have you brought back this time?"

Dreadnought gave him a long, thoughtful look. Then he said softly, "Keep it to yourselves—eight."

The seniors exchanged shocked glances. When a Blade died his sword was returned to Ironhall to hang for evermore among the thousands of others in the great sky of swords. Elderly, retired Blades—the knights in the Order—died off all the time, but not at that rate, not eight in only two months!

"Well?" Dreadnought said mockingly. "Anyone want to chicken out? If you're going to turn yellow, you'd better do it now, while the going is good—run for the hills!"

Nobody moved.

"No cowards here!" Orvil said proudly.

Rejected

As THE SUN ROSE OVER THE BARREN HILLS OF Starkmoor, Grand Master sent for the five most senior candidates. That meant only four would be bound, which was what Stalwart had dreaded.

The Flea Room was a small, bleak chamber that most boys saw only twice in all their years in Ironhall. Each newcomer met Grand Master there, and usually had to listen while whoever had brought him explained what a useless and ungrateful brat he was, and how nobody could do anything with him. Grand Master would hear the story, then talk with the boy in private and test his agility by throwing coins for him to catch. In most cases, he sent the boy and his guardian away and that was the end of it.

But if the boy had spirit and was nimble, Grand Master would accept him as a candidate. He was encouraged to take a new name and make a new person of himself. Whatever he had done in the past was forgotten. He would not see the Flea Room again unless he were set to clean it as a punishment. That was far from the worst that could happen to him, for Ironhall discipline was hard.

Time changed boys into young men. Ironhall's expert training plus a dash or two of magic turned the unwanted rebel into one of the finest swordsmen in the world. After five years or so, when the transformation was complete, the King would either accept him into the Royal Guard or assign him as bodyguard to someone else. It was back in the Flea Room that he learned his fate and met his future ward.

A companion in the Order was addressed as "Sir," although that was only a politeness, so tomorrow *Sir* Orvil, *Sir* Panther, *Sir* Dragon, *Sir* Rufus, but still only *Candidate* Stalwart . . . *sigh*!

At the door, Dreadnought took away their swords, because only a bound Blade could go armed into the King's presence. He sent them in by seniority: Orvil striding ahead, Panther close on his heels. Dragon and Rufus followed eagerly, like puppies wanting to romp. The reject trailed along behind, keeping his face blank to hide his disappointment.

There was no shame in being young, but why did it have to go on so long?

An icy wind blew off the moor, in one unglazed window and out the other. The five lined up facing Grand Master, who stood hunched in front of the inner door, clutching his cloak around him against the chill. With nine persons present, the room was crowded. The one staying out of sight at their backs would be Commander Bandit. The huge man in the corner was King Ambrose, but they must pretend not to notice him until they were instructed otherwise. He had set his hands on his hips and was grinning like a stuffed shark. His fingers glittered with jewels.

Orvil spoke the traditional words: "You sent for us, Grand Master?" He said them very loudly, so perhaps he was less calm than he was managing to appear.

"I did summon you, Prime. His Majesty has need of a Blade. Are you ready to serve?" Grand Master's beady eyes were set in a craggy, gloomy face. His name, although nobody used it, was Saxon. He was a distant, coldhearted man, inclined to lose his temper and lash out with harsh punishments, even expelling boys without fair warning. Since expulsion meant the culprit walked away over the moors with nothing but the clothes on his back—and usually no home or family to go to—it might easily be a death sentence. Even some of the elderly knights who dawdled away their final years at Ironhall would shake their heads at times and mutter that the Order had known better Grand Masters than Sir Saxon.

"I am ready, Grand Master," Orvil said quickly.

Grand Master turned and bowed. "Your Majesty, I have the honor of presenting Prime Candidate Orvil."

Now everyone could take notice of the King. Speed being more important than brawn to a swordsman, Master of Rituals used sorcery to prevent any boy growing too big. That rule did not apply to kings, though, and Ambrose IV, King of Chivial, was tall, wide, and portly. Between the calves bulging in his silk hose and the ostrich plume in his floppy hat, everything he wore seemed to be pleated and padded as if intended to make him appear even larger—knee breeches, doublet, jerkin, and fur-trimmed cloak. He loomed like a cheerful storm cloud and his voice thundered in the little room.

"Welcome to our Guard, Prime! Grand Master speaks highly of your skills."

Then Grand Master was lying. Stalwart could beat Orvil every time with rapiers and usually with sabers. Orvil would always win at broadswords, of course, because a broadsword needed more muscle than Stalwart's body had yet gotten around to providing.

Orvil bowed low, then went forward to kneel before the King and kiss his hand. As he rose to return to his place in line, Grand Master turned to Panther.

"Second, His Majesty has need of a Blade. Are you ready to serve?"

And so on. Panther was a decent man and good with steel. After him it was Dragon's turn. Dragon was only a month older than Stalwart, but looked at least eighteen. What hurt was that he fenced like a crippled cow. Master of Sabers had told him in public that he needed two more years' tuition. Deputy Master of Rapiers muttered under his breath that he ought to chop wood for a living. Yet he was going to be bound and Stalwart wasn't. No justice . . . !

"Candidate Rufus . . ."

Rufus was all right. His fencing was competent, although he was horribly predictable. Being predictable would not matter in a real fight against opponents who did not know his quirks. Besides, Rufus was nineteen and sported a beard like a gorse bush. Rufus would look convincing in Guard livery. Even Dragon would. But Stalwart . . . *sigh!* That was the trouble—not age, not competence, just looks.

Tonight at midnight there would be sorcery in the Forge. Spirits of all eight elements would be conjured. Each of the four candidates would swear his oath and—unless the magic went wrong, which it almost never did—the sword wound would heal instantly, no harm done. Then he would be a Blade.

Not only would Stalwart have to share the day-long fast and the cold baths that began the

ritual, he would also have to assist in the cere-
mony. That was adding insult to injury. When
it was over and the lucky four rode off to court,
he would remain behind as Prime, and that was
adding *injury* to injury. Prime's job was to
mother all the other boys and keep them from
pestering the masters. Being Prime was always
described as an honor, but it was an honor nobody ever wanted, communal nose drying and
butt wiping.

"Finally, sire," Grand Master bleated, "I have
the honor of presenting Candidate Stalwart,
who will henceforth serve Your Majesty as
Prime, here in Ironhall."

Rejected!

He had been told not to approach; he bowed
where he stood.

"Stalwart the musician," the King said.

Feeling his face flame scarlet, Stalwart stared
in dismay at the royal grin. King Ambrose was
known to have very strong likes and dislikes.
Did he disapprove of swordsmen playing lutes?

"I do play the lute a little, Your Majesty. . . ."

"So do I," Ambrose said heartily. "Nothing
wrong with lute playing. Maybe next time we
can make music together." Chuckling, he swung
around in a swirl of velvet and brocade and fur.
"Carry on, Grand Master."

Grand Master hastily opened the inner door
and stepped aside as the King swept by him,
ignoring all the bows directed at his back.

Dreadnought crossed the room to follow him.
Orvil led the candidates back the way they had
come, although his stupid grin was so broad
that it seemed unlikely to pass through the doorway.

Maybe next time, the King had said. That
might be a hint that he intended to foist Stalwart
off as a private Blade guarding some minister or
lord. Bindings were permanent. A man had only
one chance at the Guard.

"Stalwart!" said Grand Master. "Wait. I want
a word with you."

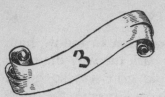

Mysterious Alternative

THE DOORS WERE CLOSED. STALWART REMAINED, with only Grand Master and Commander Bandit for company. Lacking its normal shabby furniture, the Flea Room seemed even bleaker than it had been on that dread day four years ago when Sir Vincent had brought him here and thrown him on Grand Master's mercy. It was smaller than he remembered.

"My commiserations, Candidate," Grand Master said with a mawkish smile. He glanced briefly at Commander Bandit, who was staying back, out of the conversation. Then he pouted at Stalwart. Obviously he was in one of his crabbiest moods. "Had I put the question to you, how would you have answered? Would you be willing to serve?"

"Of course, Grand Master!" Why would he be there if he did not intend to become a Blade? Why would he be putting up with constant

14

sneers and browbeating from Grand Master? Four years . . .

"It is unfortunate that you chose the name you did. You are not yet convincingly *stalwart*."

"It is not for lack of wishing, Grand Master."

"You have *dimples*!" Grand Master's face was spotted with ugly brown blotches. Was being young more shameful than being old?

The school would not let a candidate sacrifice speed by growing too large, but it also required that he grow to man's strength. Time and again, Stalwart had begged Master of Rituals to perform a growth sorcery on him, but every time he was refused with much the same words: "It's not size that's your problem, candidate, it's just timing. If you're still on the small side when you've got a beard to shave, then we can do something about it."

"So you are willing to serve." Grand Master gave him a look that seemed to contain equal parts contempt and pity. "How willing? Would you tell lies to serve His Majesty?"

Now what? Puzzled, Stalwart said, "After I am bound I will do absolutely anything to defend him, naturally."

"That was not what I asked. I said *serve*, not *defend*. And I am not talking about *when you are bound*. I mean now. Would you lie to a friend if the King ordered you to do so?" Why was he so cantankerous this morning? Why take it out on Stalwart?

"I can't believe King Ambrose would ever give me such an order, sir."

"Can't you? Oh, grow up, boy! Suppose I tell you that you could best serve His Majesty by kicking up dust . . . jumping the hill . . . disappearing. . . . Does your loyalty extend that far?"

In this game to show anger was to lose points. A man could never win when Grand Master chose to pick on him like this, but he could play to a draw by remaining calm and courteous. That was rarely easy.

"With all respect, sir, I should not believe you."

"I assure you that this is His Majesty's wish." Grand Master's smile came very close to being a sneer. "And if you are going to call me a liar, the Commander will confirm what I say."

Dismayed, Stalwart looked to Sir Bandit, who shrugged.

"What Grand Master says is true, Candidate, but he is not telling you the whole story."

Grand Master sniffed. "The story's your business. I don't know it and I don't want to know. Stalwart, I was told to tell you that the Commander speaks with the King's knowledge and approval. That's all."

He strode over to the inner door and shut it behind him with a thump that was very close to a slam. Bandit did not comment, but he rolled his eyes just enough to convey his opinion of that show of temper. Stalwart was duly grateful.

Bandit himself could hardly have been a more different person. Not in looks, of course. In appearance he was a typical Blade—graceful, athletic, neither tall nor short. His only remarkable feature was the way his eyebrows joined to make a single dark hedge across his face. He wore neither beard nor mustache. According to rumor, the Commander was one of the worst fencers in the entire Guard. There had been widespread surprise last Firstmoon when the King chose him to replace the legendary Sir Durendal, but he had proved to be an excellent choice. He had infinite patience. He spoke to the greenest recruit in exactly the same tone and manner he used to the King. His sword was named *Suasion*.

He walked over to the nearer window and stared out at the moor. "This is to be in confidence, every word."

"Yes, Commander."

"You were surprised that the King knew about your lute playing."

"Surprised that it interested him. I suppose Grand Master described all the seniors to him this morning?"

Bandit turned to share a smile. "He did not have to. He sends me detailed reports on all of you every week. I pass them on when the King wants to see them. He has been following your progress ever since you were promoted from fuzzy, last Thirdmoon.''

"Oh!"

"He knows you've been here not quite four years and you won't be seventeen till Tenthmoon. He has seen Grand Master's reports describing you as lazy, insubordinate, and disliked by both the masters and the other boys.''

Stunned, Stalwart said nothing.

Bandit continued: "Over the last two months he has become increasingly critical. He describes your fencing as very bad, virtually hopeless.''

That was too much! *"Sir!* I suggest you ask the others. Master of Rapiers—"

"Says you can beat him nine times out of ten." The Commander was smiling again. "Not half an hour ago, Grand Master assured the King to his face that you are diligent, courteous, and industrious. He said no one was better liked, and no one showed more promise or ability at fencing. Does that make you feel better?"

"I hope that's closer to the truth, sir." Not at all bad, either! *No one better liked! Wow!*

"You can't possibly have had enough spare time here to learn how to play a lute. You must have brought it with you?"

"I was almost hanged for stealing it."

The Commander's long eyebrow arched in surprise, then he smiled. "Your past is your business. It's your present and future that interest me. You've turned out to be a late bloomer.

It's no fault of yours and normally wouldn't matter. You'll get there in time; we all do. But, as Grand Master says, your chosen name does tend to draw attention to your current lack of stature." On Grand Master's lips the comment had been a sneer. When Sir Bandit said it, it was sympathy.

"Yes, sir. *Puny* would have been a better choice."

"I don't think the King would ever admit a *Sir Puny* to his Guard." The Commander eyed him thoughtfully for a moment. "Don't worry! It will come. And 'stalwart' doesn't just mean 'big and strong.' It also means 'brave and reliable.' That's the stalwart I need."

The man in question drew a deep breath to soothe the sudden turmoil in his insides. "*Yes,* Commander?"

"You won't know this, but this Grand Master has been forbidden to expel anyone else without the King's permission—no one wants Ironhall-trained men running around the country with chips on their shoulders. In his written reports, he has twice asked leave to . . . in my day we called it *puke* you. Throw you out, I mean."

Aware that the Commander was waiting for his reaction, Stalwart took a moment to think. Why should Grand Master write nonsense to Sir Bandit and the King, then turn around and tell them the truth in person? "He was *ordered* to write that trash about me? Who else reads it? Spies?"

"Well done! Yes, spies. Maybe spies—we're not sure. You know the evil we are up against—"

"Not exactly, sir."

The Commander turned and began to pace. "I mean you know about as much as we do. Counting the Night of Dogs there have been four attempts on the King's life in the last eight months, yes?"

"Yes, sir."

"No. There have been ten, four in the last month. That number is a state secret, Stalwart. No one outside the Guard knows that total, not even King Ambrose himself. You won't repeat it to anyone!"

"No, Commander." Stalwart thought his voice sounded a little thinner than usual.

"Obviously we don't know who the conspirators are or we'd hack their hearts out. Obviously they include some powerful sorcerers, and the attacks began when the King asked Parliament to levy taxes on the elementaries and conjuring orders. He saw no reason why wealthy organizations like those shouldn't pay their share like everyone else. Some of them disagreed. Now he's formed the Court of Conjury to investigate the uses of magic in his kingdom and it's turning up horrible evils. This is open war, Candidate—*and we don't know who the enemy is!*" Bandit returned to the window and stared out, probably seeing nothing. The King's safety rested on his shoulders.

"We aren't certain that the villains have eyes and ears at court, but it's a reasonable guess that they do. The only people we Blades trust are ourselves. Our binding keeps us loyal. We can deal with anything mortal, whether it's human or a monster created by magic. We have tasters for the King's food—and two of them have died. When it comes to secret sorcery we must rely on the White Sisters to sniff it out for us." The Commander swung around to stare at Stalwart. "I'll let you into another secret—just last week one of the Sisters detected something suspicious in the royal laundry. We burned the whole lot of it. Another smelled sorcery in the stables and tracked it to the King's favorite saddle. So you see that the evil extends right inside Greymere Palace."

For a moment, Bandit looked old and worried. Then he smiled and was young again. "Don't worry—Ambrose knows how you use a sword and he does want you in his Guard. Of course in normal times you'd have a dozen seniors still ahead of you, so you may not be quite as blazing good as you think you are. No matter, you are very good. The trouble is this absurd rule about taking men in order of seniority. There are good men coming along behind you, men like Badger and Marlon. I need those men. Forgive me, but I just can't see you in a Guard uniform yet."

Sigh! again. "I'd look about fourteen, wouldn't I?" Courtiers would make jokes about make-believe and children's pageants.

Bandit shrugged.

"Twelve?"

The Commander laughed, but not unkindly. "Not quite that bad! I'm glad you understand. Six months ought to do it. In the meantime I've got another job that you can do for the King, an important job. A risky job. He's given me authority to swear you into the Guard without binding you. Are you willing to serve?"

But the rules said . . . Stalwart realized that he was standing there like a lummox with his mouth open. "*Yes, sir!*"

"Are you certain?" Bandit asked quietly. "This is where I need that brave-and-reliable Stalwart. It will be dangerous. A Blade never needs to worry about courage, because his binding makes him brave." His eyes seemed to go out of focus. "On the Night of Dogs . . . some of those monsters were big as horses. They climbed three stories up the outside of the palace and came in the windows at us. They chewed through steel bars. They fought until they were hacked to pieces—*and so did the Blades!* I saw men with an arm bitten off pick up their swords in their other hand and go on fighting. A Blade defending his ward is more than human." He blinked and came back to the present. "I hope you won't have to face anything so bad, but you won't have that motivation."

Stalwart had been shown some of the gigantic teeth that Blades had kept as souvenirs. He shivered. "No, sir."

"And here's another secret. Some of the knights . . . well, let's just say they did not live up to the traditions of the Order. Not being bound any longer, they had to rely on raw human courage, and one or two of them didn't quite measure up."

Blades running away? Stalwart was speechless.

"That night was just the start of it," Bandit said. "There have been other horrors since. Twenty-four Blades have died so far—eight knights and sixteen companions. A score have been badly injured, and I've lost count of civilian casualties. We're not calling this the Monster War for nothing. Are you stalwart enough, Candidate Stalwart? Can you take on a dangerous job without being bound?"

He hadn't yet said what the job was. Apparently the planning had been going on for months and the King himself had authorized it. It must be important. Stalwart's heart thundered in his throat.

"I'll try my best, sir."

"I can't ask for more. Come with me."

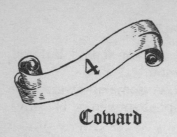

Coward

BANDIT LED THE WAY DOWNSTAIRS, UPSTAIRS, through the maze of corridors. First House was the oldest building in Ironhall, much of it dating back centuries. Now Stalwart had time to have some second thoughts—and a few third thoughts, too. What exactly had he been flattered into accepting? Was it necessarily better than being assigned to guard the Lord High Admiral or the Master of the King's Chicken Farms? That was what happened to the dregs; only the best were allowed into the Guard.

So he looked too young to appear in Blade livery—why did that stop his being bound with the others? They could take him to court and dress him like a page if they wanted. What he was being offered instead was a major breach of the rules—and if the King had approved it, then why wasn't the King saying so? A binding ritual could not begin before midnight, so Ambrose had all day to kill. It had to be the royal hand on the sword that bound a Blade, but was Stalwart so much less than the others that he couldn't be spared a few minutes? Or did the King not want to be involved?

Bandit strode into the Records Office without knocking. Master of Archives stood at his writing desk under the window, surrounded by his usual wilderness of clutter. Heaps of scrolls and piles of great leather books filled the shelves, the chairs, and the floor, leaving nowhere to sit and precious little room to stand. He was stooped and perpetually untidy, with hair mussed and eyeglasses settled on the very tip of his nose. Even this day when everyone was spruced up for the King's visit, he seemed ink stained, shabby, and dog-eared. Yet the cat's-eye sword dangling at his side showed he was still a knight in the Order.

"Good chance, Lester!" the Commander said cheerily. Stalwart had never known, or even wondered, what the archivist's name was. "Need you to witness and record something." He fished a thin roll out of his jerkin and separated it into two sheets of paper. "File this. It's a warrant promoting Candidate Stalwart to companion, no binding required."

Master of Archives peered at it, holding it almost at the end of his nose. "I never heard of such a thing! In three hundred years there has never—"

"There is now," Bandit said cheerfully.

"That's the royal signet. Fat Man is head of the Order and this matter is within the royal prerogative. You going to argue with him?" He handed the other paper to Stalwart. "Close the door, lad. Read that out."

The text was very brief, closely matching the oath sworn when a Blade was bound to the King:

Upon my soul, I, Stalwart, companion in the Loyal and Ancient Order of the King's Blades, do irrevocably swear in the presence of the undersigned, my brethren, that I will evermore defend His Majesty King Ambrose IV, his heirs and successors, against all foes, setting my own life as nothing to shield him from peril. Done this fifth day of Eighthmoon, in the three hundred and sixty-eighth year of the House of Ranulf.

"Now sign it. May he borrow your quill, Lester? Add 'companion' after your name. Congratulations, Sir Stalwart!"

Master of Archives was making spluttering sounds like an annoyed goose. "That is absolutely outrageous!"

"We live in strange times." Bandit took the pen to write "Witnessed Bandit, Commander," under Stalwart's admittedly shaky signature, then handed it to Master of Archives. "Now you, Lester. File it somewhere very secure, and enter Sir Stalwart's name in the rolls."

"B-b-but . . ."

"The records must be correct, because there will be false stories spread." Bandit turned to regard Stalwart, compressing his long eyebrow in a frown. "Your sword's ready, of course, but you can't have it today. We'll try to get it to you. What's her name to be?"

Things were happening too fast. "Sleight, sir." Stalwart had said it before he realized that—*if* all this was for real, and *if* he didn't come out of it alive—the sword Sleight might be hung in the sky of swords before he had ever seen her or laid hands on her. "Not 'slight.' 'Sleight,' like sleight of hand."

The Commander chuckled. "Good one! I'll have Master Armorer inscribe it. Write that in your book also, Lester. Well, that's all, *Sir* Stalwart! Welcome to the Royal Guard." He offered a handshake.

"Th-thank you, er, Leader." Stalwart was miserably aware that his own palm was sweaty. He dearly wanted to ask why he wasn't being bound, but he feared he would not like the answer.

"Glad to have you. Here are your first orders. Go straight to your quarters. Gather up whatever you own, including that lute of yours, and then go."

"Go, sir?"

"Out. What was it Grand Master said—kick up dust? Must have been catchy talk fifty years ago. Walk out the gate. Take the Lomouth road and keep going. Someone'll be waiting for you at Broom Tarn."

The Commander's steady stare was a challenge to steady the new recruit's fluttering insides. Not just butterflies in the stomach—he had bats in the belly. A Blade could not refuse an order, but it was very obvious that he might have fallen into some sort of elaborate trap. Suppose there *wasn't* someone waiting for him on the road? Where would he go, what could he do?

"Yes, sir."

Bandit smiled to acknowledge what those two little words had cost. "I'll be at the gate to see you get past the Blades there."

"Thank you, sir!" He was to be given no breakfast?

"But if anyone asks you where you're going, you will not answer."

"Sir?"

The Commander shrugged. "Has to be, Stalwart. Despite what Grand Master said, I won't ask you to lie to your friends. I hope you can't, because it's not an ability to be proud of. And you mustn't tell the truth. If there truly are spies back at court, they'll assume you got puked because you're a lousy fencer. People here in Ironhall will know better than that, but they'll assume the old man lost his temper with you. Or you annoyed the King, or something."

No, they would assume he'd lost his nerve and run away. He was going to be branded a coward.

Bandit did not say that, though. "Believe me, this is *very* important! We can't protect you where you're going, you see. If one careless word lets the enemy suspect that you matter, then you're as good as dead. So today you refuse to talk. Understand?"

"I'll obey orders, sir," Stalwart said hoarsely.

"Good man!" The Commander forestalled his questions with a head shake. "Don't ask. The man at Broom Tarn will explain. I don't dare tell you more now. Officially you've been expelled."

"Yes, Leader." Stalwart turned and went.

The instant the door closed behind him, Master of Archives said, "Well you can dare tell me! What is all this nonsense? What's going on?"

Bandit had his eyes closed. He let out a long, long breath, as if he'd been holding it for a week. "No, I can't tell you."

"I don't like this!"

"Neither do I."

"Spirits, Leader, that boy's only a . . . a . . . a *child*! Did you see how his chin trembled?"

The Commander opened his eyes and scowled. "Yes, I did. Did you see how he obeyed orders in spite of it?"

"You're sending a child into mortal danger!" Master of Archives yelled. "You're bound. You've forgotten what fear is like. I tell you, the week after I was dubbed knight and unbound I got into a fight and suddenly my hand was shaking so—"

The Commander's fist flashed out and grabbed the older man's jerkin. His eyes blazed. "Don't push too far, Lester! I've told you I don't like it. And you will not breathe one word of this to anyone, you hear? *Nobody!* Give me your oath on it."

"I swear, Leader."

"I'll hold you to it." Bandit released him.

Sir Lester restored his dignity by straightening his jerkin, like a chicken rearranging its feathers. "Is this Snake's doing? Is that who's he going to meet—Snake?"

"Snake or one of his men."

"You really think that . . . that *boy* . . . is going to do any good?"

The Commander turned and picked his way across the littered floor. "I can't tell you. I don't know what's going on either. Snake and the King dreamed it up. Maybe Durendal was in on it—I don't know. I do know that we've lost far too many men and Ambrose's luck can't last forever." With his hand on the latch he looked back. "I'm desperate, Lester. I'll try anything."

"Because all you're risking is one boy with no father to complain and no mother to mourn!"

"That's all," Bandit said harshly. "One starry-eyed boy. Lots more where he came from."

A Fateful Scream

TWO DAYS LATER, A STAGECOACH CAME RUM-
bling through Tyton, a town in eastern Chivial.
It stopped at the Gatehouse, the entry to Oakendown, headquarters of the Companionship of
the White Sisters, who were commonly known
as *sniffers*, because they were trained to detect
magic.

If the Monster War had put the King's Blades
into a state of simmering alert, it had brought
the Sisters to a wild boil. In normal times about
twenty-five of them lived at court, assisting the
Royal Guard in its duties. Another two hundred
or so worked for nobles or rich merchants, and
the rest were mostly teachers at Oakendown.
Now the Blades were demanding the services of
every Sister they could get. So were the nobles
and merchants. Hundreds more people who had
never given a thought to the dangers of evil
magic had been alarmed by the Night of Dogs
and were howling for Sisters to protect them.

Probably few of them realized that a Sister could do no more than detect the presence of magic. Even other sorcerers could rarely defend against it.

At the best of times there were never enough Sisters. Only girls who were naturally sensitive and compassionate were accepted. They were taught courtly manners and given an excellent education—which was unusual in Chivial, where very few women knew even the rudiments of reading. Suitors pursued the Sisters like bees after blossoms. More than half of them were married within two years of taking their oaths. In the Monster War emergency, Mother Superior had appealed to all former Sisters to return to service. Many had done so, but there were still not nearly enough to satisfy the demand. Every prioress in the country was hunting for suitable recruits.

The stagecoach had brought six. They were met at the gatehouse by a young woman in the sparkling white robes and tall conical hat of a White Sister. She told them her name was Emerald and she would be their guide in their first few months at Oakendown. She did not mention that she had been a mere deaconess until the previous day. As she had not been due to take her vows for another three months and had been given only an hour's notice of her promotion, she had not yet quite adjusted to her new status. She was also still convinced that the hennin was about to fall off her head at any moment, but she didn't mention that either.

"Your names I do not want to know," she added, and smiled at their surprise. "Later I'll explain why. Meanwhile, I am sure you are tired and probably hungry. Which need do you want to satisfy first?" The vote was unanimous. She led them to the refectory to eat.

In the great hall under the high rafters, they gazed around with wide eyes while stuffing themselves with roast venison and rich fruit pudding. Especially they stared at passing Sisters.

"When do we get to wear the funny hats?" asked one, braver than the rest.

"When you finish your training. In about four years." It might be nearer three, Emerald suspected, if the present demand continued. She pointed out postulants like themselves, also novices, and deaconesses. "This is where we touch the world," she said. "On that side lies Tyton, and through this door, across the bridge, is the real Oakendown. We come to the gatehouse to eat sometimes, but not always. It is a busy place, as you can see. Merchants come here to sell things to us. Persons who wish to contract for our services come here. If members of your family come to visit you, then you will meet them here. Outsiders are not allowed to cross the stream. See those people with hair on their faces? They are called 'men'!" The girls all laughed, of course. "Take a good look, because you won't see any of those on the other side of Oakenburn." The reasons for that involved one of the virtual elements and a lecture she would save for another day.

Meanwhile, her young charges seemed to be accepting her. Half a dozen scared, excited twelve- or thirteen-year-olds were quite a handful for someone only four years older, but she was an earth person and well able to cope. By the time the six were so full that they could not stuff in one more mouthful between them, she had won their trust. She took them to Wardrobe and saw them outfitted in postulants' brown robes. She explained that their own clothes would be given away to the poor.

"Suppose we want to go home?" wailed one of the air children.

"You can always go home, and we shall give you clothes to wear. Do you think we would put you in the coach naked?"

They laughed nervously. She had them classified now—one earth, one water, one fire, and three air. Every person's disposition contained all four of the manifest elements, of course, but one of the four was always dominant. Similarly, one of the four virtual elements would prevail: time, chance, love, or death. Those were a little harder to distinguish. Being an earth-time person, Emerald was solid, methodical, and patient. She was also heavy boned, destined for plumpness within very few years, and her broad features would never inspire poets to sonnets. "Comely" would be the most charitable epithet ever applied to them. Oakendown had taught her to accept what the spirits had brought her and not to fret. Her six nestlings were seeing her as trustworthy and motherly, which was undoubtedly why she had been assigned as a guide.

The sun was close to setting when she led her charges through the gate and over the footbridge that spanned the Oakenburn. She was always happy to leave the world's unfamiliar turmoil and return to the peace of the forest. Some Sisters remained in Oakendown all their lives, and she might turn out to be one of them if she did a good job guiding these six. It would not be so terrible a fate.

"Oakendown is very big, and I will need several days to show you all of it."

"Why do you live in trees?" squeaked one of the air types.

"Do we get to live up there?" another cried excitedly.

"Do we *have* to?" moaned the earth child.

They all peered up at the cabins nestling in the branches, the long bridges slung from tree to tree.

"Shush!" Emerald said gently. "You must *never* shout in Oakendown!" Time enough tomorrow to explain that postulants should rarely speak at all. "Yes, tonight you will sleep up in a tree. It is a very cozy, pleasant cabin, I promise you, and it doesn't sway at all. Later you will live in other places. There are lakes with many little islands and houseboats. There are caves—"

"*Caves?*" wailed the three air and one fire. The earth and water children smiled excitedly.

"Yes, caves. You have to learn to recognize the flow of the spirits. All your lives you have been in contact with earth elementals. Up in a tree, you are removed from them. In a cave, you are away from air—as far as you can be without suffocating. And also from fire, although we don't make you freeze to death. Gradually you come to sense the presence or absence of the various spirits. It isn't as difficult as it sounds."

It was a slow process, though, and not without hardship. Spending days underground was taxing for an air person; only a fire child could enjoy standing for hours under a blazing sun.

As they walked deeper into the forest, she mentioned that oaks were the only trees that extended their limbs horizontally. She pointed out how cunningly the aerial platforms were braced on those great boughs. When they reached their home tree she showed them the inconspicuous number written on the first riser of the wooden stair twining upward around the great trunk. This was Tree 65 of First Grove. Then she told them to go and explore. The three air girls went racing up ahead.

The earth child stuck close to Emerald. *Bounty* might be a good name for her. Her dominant virtual was almost certainly love, and with that combination her destiny was to marry young and produce children by the dozen.

Sixty-five was a juvenile tree by Oakendown standards. Its boughs held only a dormitory for the postulants, a private room higher up for their guide, a few meditation nests in the upper branches, and the necessary toilet facilities. No bridges connected it to other trees.

"Postulants are not allowed candles in the tree houses," Emerald explained, "so you get ready for bed now and then we'll talk." She watched to see how they settled the distribution of the pallets—who argued, who acquiesced.

Fire spirits had faded with the day, but the night was hot. She opened all the dormitory windows, sensing the air elementals rustling the leaves of the forest canopy. Then she gathered her little brood together in the deepening gloom as if she were going to tell them all a bedtime story, which in a sense she was. With all seven of them sitting cross-legged in a circle, she bade them hold hands, remembering her own first night in Oakendown and Sister Cloud doing this.

"Now you are among friends, in a very safe place. You can sleep soundly. Do not chatter in bed, because that is unkind to others. Dawn comes soon and the birds will rouse you, but I promised to answer any—"

Two of the air children tried to speak and the fire child drowned them out. "Why wouldn't you let us tell you our names?"

It was the question she had expected to come first. "Because in a day or two we are going to choose new names for each of you. I want you to try and forget your old names. I address each of you as 'Postulant,' and I want you to speak to one another that way, too. We won't force you to accept a name you don't like. When I came here I was given the name of Emerald and I soon realized that it was a much better name for me than the one my mother gave me. How could she know when I was born what sort of person I would turn out to be? No, Postulant, I will *not* tell you what it was, and you should not interrupt when I am speaking."

It had been *Lucy Pillow*, and she was still trying to forget it.

"If you later decide that the name we have chosen for you is wrong, then you may ask to change it. Names are words and words have power. It is with words that sorcerers bind the elementals, and some people are bound by their own names. We must find you names that express your true natures so they do not restrict you, that is all. What else?"

"What does magic smell like?" That query

came from the little air child Emerald was already thinking of as *Wren*, although of course the Mistress of Postulants would have to approve her choices. The water child would probably be something like *Snowflake*. Water people were diverse and notoriously changeable, but this one already had an astonishing beauty, bright and cold. If her dominant virtual was death, as Emerald suspected, then she was going to shatter men's hearts like icicles. No matter how well-meaning death people might be, they were destructive to others and often to themselves as well.

She laughed. "I can't tell you. You have to experience it, and every Sister seems to experience it differently. It isn't really a smell. Often it's more a sound or a feeling." But it could be a smell, especially when air elementals were much involved. She sniffed . . .

Oh, nonsense! Just talking about it was making her imagine . . . There were places in Oakendown where sorceries were performed, of course. Once the novices had learned to recognize the natural flow of the spirits, they had to be taught the distorted forms produced by magic. But never in the groves.

And yet she could almost swear . . .

"Tell us about the Monster War."

Emerald wanted to say that she knew no more than they did, but perhaps they really did not know much. Wharshire was a long way from the center. News might be badly distorted by the time it arrived there.

"Do you all know what an elementary is?"

"A place for healing!"

"It can be. The place where sorcerers invoke the spirits is properly called an octogram, the eight-pointed star marked on the ground, but people do use the word 'elementary' to mean the building containing it. It can also mean the group or organization that owns the building, the *conjuring order*. They perform healings, yes, but they may do other things as well. Lately many conjuring orders have grown very rich, buying up land. They've begun putting on airs, too—the House of This and the Priory of That. . . . Last winter, the King decided the elementaries ought to pay taxes like other people do. Some wicked sorcerers banded together and tried to kill the King. They sent monsters—"

"Dogs big as horses—"

"Packs of them eating people in the palace—"

"Shush, shush!" Just when she had been getting them calmed down! "I'm sure the stories were exaggerated. Anyway, His Majesty set up a Court of Conjury, which is investigating all the conjuring orders and elementaries. Some of them do good, but many have turned out to be very wicked. They sell curses and bewitch people into giving them money. It's created a lot of worry about evil sorcery and that's why everyone suddenly wants a White Sister around. You will learn how to play your part. Now are you ready for bed, because . . ."

The stench was becoming nauseating, suggesting to Emerald huge quantities of rotting meat. Not being attuned to magic yet, her companions were noticing nothing amiss. But there must be qualified Sisters in some of the nearby trees, and they should be within range of anything this powerful. Anyone conjuring spirits right here in First Grove ought to have raised a hullabaloo audible in the next county.

She disentangled herself and stood up. "You get into bed. I'll be back in just a minute." She headed for the door.

Out on the platform, she could hear faint voices from neighboring trees, so she was not alone in the forest; she could see a few lights. Yet the stench of magic was even worse than before. She could detect air and death and a hint of time, but the combination felt gruesome and evil. She stood in the still night, almost gagging on it, barely able to concentrate well enough to try and locate it. It must be very close, perhaps right in this very tree. There was nothing below her, just the stair. Above her the steps went on, winding up to higher branches and the smaller huts.

Suddenly she saw the glint of eyes, too many eyes, up in the bracing that supported her sleeping cabin. A magical creation could be just as real and just as dangerous as any natural peril.

When it saw that she had seen it, it came at her, scampering down out of the dark—a spider the size of a sheepdog with outspread legs like cables, mandibles big as daggers, eight eyes shining. It came on a wave of sorcery that was absolutely mind breaking.

Fire people might scream with rage, water people with fear, and air people just for the sake of the noise, but Emerald had always believed that earth people never screamed. She was wrong. She screamed at the top of her lungs. She hurled herself back into the dormitory, still screaming, and slammed the door against the horror outside. The six postulants, already very perturbed, quite understandably panicked. Three of them leaped out windows. A moment later came the sickening thump of a body hitting the ground.

Sentence

LATE THE FOLLOWING MORNING, SISTER EMER-
ald was released from the meditation cell in
which she had been confined overnight. She was
led across the grove by way of many trees and
bridges, coming at last to a large, mossy building set very high in one of the great forest giants.
The tree was centuries old, and its buildings
looked almost as ancient. She was taken to a gra-
cious, dignified room, furnished with antiques,
lined with ancient books. On this hot summer
day it was cool and pleasant, bearing a homely
smell of lavender and beeswax. Her guides—or
perhaps they were jailers—showed her in without a word and then departed, leaving her alone
with a white-robed woman, who sat writing at
the big desk.

Emerald sank to her knees on the threadbare
rug and waited as she had been taught, with
hands clasped and eyes downcast. After a few
moments of silence, she dared to glance up. She

44

had expected the Prioress, but this was Mother Superior herself, the head of the Companionship. There could be no appeal from whatever verdict was to be announced here.

Eventually the older woman replaced her quill in the silver inkstand and sat back to frown at her visitor. She wasted no time on pleasantries. "I have read your entire file, Sister—every report on you in the last four years. Your record is impressive. You were an exemplary student. I have also read the statement you gave last night, and that makes no sense whatsoever. Do you wish to recant?"

Mother Superior's control was the most perfect Emerald had ever met. Even here, high up in the ancient, enduring tree, with only insubstantial spirits of air and time around, any slight traces of the other elements should be as obvious as flying camels, and yet the lady was revealing no imbalances at all. She might be an earth person, or water, or fire, but Emerald could not venture a guess.

"I spoke only the truth, mistress."

Mother Superior drummed fingers on the desk. "Magic? Giant spiders conjured in the middle of Oakendown? This is rubbish! Nobody but you sensed anything at all, child. A dozen Sisters were so close to your location that they could not have missed detecting what you claim. So monstrous a sorcery must leave a taint that would linger for days, yet our most expert sniffers can find no trace of one. What you are claiming is rank impossibility!"

Someone was lying. Perhaps many people. Something terrible had happened in Oakendown and truth had been among the slain.

"May I speak with some of these reverend ladies?"

Mother Superior stiffened as if she could not believe her ears. "Are you accusing me of lying to you?"

"No, mistress." She was, of course. "But *I* am being accused—of falsehood or insanity or something. Do I not have the right to face my accusers?"

"There are no accusers," Mother Superior said menacingly. "Except me. Now, will you recant this absurd nonsense?"

Alas, Emerald had not been so named without reason. An emerald was a very hard jewel. The earth-time disposition was always marked by extreme stubbornness. "I regret I cannot tell a lie, my lady."

She met the angry stare and held it until Mother Superior reddened and looked away. Fingers drummed again. The decision was made.

Before it could be announced, Emerald said, "May I ask how the children are?"

"The one who fell will survive. At worst she will have a slight limp. However she required such extensive healing that there can be no hope of her ever joining the Companionship. The others suffered a very considerable fright and are being counseled."

"I am truly sorry for what happened to them. I deeply regret my weakness in giving in to panic, but—"

Mother Superior pursed old lips. "If you had truly seen what you said you saw, then nobody would blame you for panicking." That was almost an offer of a second chance.

"I did see it, and I cannot say otherwise."

"Then I have no choice but to expel you from the Companionship. As is our custom, we shall provide transportation back to wherever you were recruited. You will be granted room and board until arrangements are made."

Emerald rose. Proper decorum required that she now curtsey, back up three steps, curtsey again. Angrily she just spun around and marched to the door.

Trials

THE NEXT FEW DAYS WERE THE MOST MISERABLE of her life. She was cut off from the only world and friends she had known for the last four years, abandoned in the heartless confusion of Tyton, outside even the familiar gatehouse. She had no money and nothing to do. Once or twice she saw Sisters she knew going about the Companionship's business in the town, but she could not bear to approach them in case they spurned her—or worse—offered sympathy.

Each dawn and sunset she had to report to the clerks at the gatehouse door. This involved joining a shoving, elbow-jabbing scrum with a hundred other people to reach the tables and a shouting match when she got there. Once a clerk had established that no transportation had yet been assigned to her, he would give her a token to exchange for food at a tavern. The food at Peter's was worse than the food at the Silver Hind, which was much worse than the Acorn's,

and that was fit only for pigs. The fine fare of
the refectory was not available to outsiders,
which is what she now was. Gone, too, were the
soft white robes. The drab gown and bonnet that
she had been given in their stead were coarse
and shapeless. The shoes pinched her feet.

Worst of all was the bitter taste of injustice.
Something very wrong had happened in Oakendown that night. She *knew* she had detected a
genuine magic; she was quite certain that
Mother Superior knew she had. Others must
know it also. A postulant had been injured, five
others terrified half out of their minds, but the
elaborate denial showed that much worse events
must be involved. If Emerald were not so im-
placably stubborn she would have joined the
chorus of liars and been spared this unfair ban-
ishment. On the second morning, when she saw
the southbound stage leaving with half its seats
empty, she realized that this was still what she
was expected to do. She was being given a
chance to write a note, begging for forgiveness
and claiming a change of memory. Alas, earth
and time were unbending rulers. Or was stubbornness only pride?

After Oakendown's serene solitude, the mill-
ing crowds seemed an unending nightmare,
haunted by a pervasive reek of magic. She could
rarely find a seat in the dining rooms without
being close to an amulet of some kind. Most of
those were merely phony good-luck charms—

useless and relatively harmless—but several men tried to strike up friendships with her using glamours. Those sorceries were intended to make their wearers irresistible, but to her trained talent the results were as repulsive as hot dung heaps. Two of her encounters with magic were more noteworthy.

On the second evening, as she was bracing herself to fight her way into the mob at the gatehouse, a sudden odor of hot metal made her spin around. She would not have been surprised to see a huckster wheeling a brazier roasting chestnuts or even a farrier bearing a red-hot horseshoe in his tongs. What she observed instead were two dapper young men in green and silver livery. Curtly, but not roughly, they were clearing a path for an older man. She guessed at once that they were Blades and what she was detecting was the binding that kept them loyal to their ward, whoever he was. As they went by her, she glimpsed the gleaming cat's-eye gems on the pommels of their swords. They had no need to draw those weapons or display their renowned skill at using them. Their self-assurance alone was enough to make the bystanders yield, and in a few moments they and their ward had been passed through the door into the reception halls beyond. Emerald had never seen Blades before and probably never would again. They were a reminder of shattered dreams, for every novice in Oakendown hoped for an assignment to court one day, and she had been no exception.

The evening meal token also bought her a place to sleep, but the inns packed their guests in two or even three to a bed, four or five beds to a room. On her first night, Emerald was last to arrive and thus had to sleep nearest the door. Her five roommates seemed to spend the entire night climbing over her to get to the chamber pot. She vowed that henceforth she would retire right after eating.

Even that precaution was not proof against misfortune. On the third night of her exile, having been assigned a berth in the Acorn, she reached the room first and claimed a snug corner. Five women followed her and settled in with the usual jokes about bedbugs and snoring. One place seemed destined to remain empty, but just as they agreed to snuff out the candle, another woman bustled in, carrying a large carpetbag.

Hearing what seemed to be a continuous note blown on a very shrill whistle, Emerald sat up. "Pardon me, mistress, but are you wearing a sorcery of some sort?"

At a guess, the matron was the wife of a prosperous merchant—large, middle-aged, and surprisingly well dressed to be residing at the Acorn. Perhaps it was the best she had been able to find with the town so full. She simpered across the beds at Emerald. "Merely a charm of good fortune."

"Mistress, you have been gulled. That is no good-luck charm."

The woman glared. "It came from the Priory of Peace at Swampham. The brothers' prices are quite outrageous, but they have a countrywide reputation."

The lady would have done better hiring the brethren's magic to improve her teeth and remove her mustache, but to say so would require considerable tact.

"I never heard of that priory, mistress, or even of Swampham. But I do know something about magic. I know that there is no such thing as a true good-luck charm. All that any sorcery can do is drive away spirits of chance. They are so fickle that such charms rarely make much difference at all, and even if they do, they will keep away good luck just as much as bad."

"She's right!" one of the other women said. "If your charm worked, goodwife, then you wouldn't be in here with us."

The others laughed.

"Ask it for a room full of handsome men-at-arms!" said another.

"Insolence!" shrieked the woman with the amulet. "Nobody asked your opinions! Mind your own business, all of you."

The sorcerous racket was Emerald's business if she hoped to sleep tonight, but she did not try to explain that. "I can't imagine what business you have at Oakendown, mistress. If you try to speak with the Sisters while wearing that horror, they won't listen to a word you say."

But the problem was Emerald's not the woman's. She dressed and went down the creaking stairs to ask the innkeeper for another berth. She was directed to another room, but the beds were already filled, so she spent the night in a grubby blanket on a dirty floor. Her roommates all snored loudly.

On the following morning, the clerk found a note beside her name. "Ah, yes . . . Lucy Pillow. Greenwood Livery Stable. Ask for the Duke of Eastfare's man."

To leave Oakendown was tragedy, but she assumed that anything would be better than this shadowy nonexistence in Tyton.

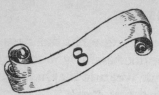

The Open Road

THAT ASSUMPTION SOON BEGAN TO SEEM RASH. In the chilly dawn, the Greenwood yard was a clanking, clattering confusion of men and horses, reeking of ammonia, messy underfoot. Enormous animals were being led around, frequently at a run. Harnesses jingled, men shouted and cursed. In among the carts, drays, and wagons stood several grand carriages, but none of the footmen or postilions attending them would admit that his outfit belonged to the Duke of Eastfare.

By a process of elimination, she eventually arrived at a large gray horse harnessed to a shabby little wagon. The fresh-faced, cheeky-looking boy holding its harness strap was peering around, frowning. When he saw her horrified eye on him he said, "Pillow?"

"You may address me as Mistress Emerald."

"And I may not." To call him a youth would be premature. His shirt, breeches, and jerkin

54

were all old and tattered, his floppy cap sat on
hair of polished straw hanging down over his
ears. He was only a finger-width taller than she
was, although he drew himself up very straight
to make the most of it. "You're the biddy going
to Newhurst? Jump in."

This was too much! "You expect me to ride in
that?" The rig had no protection from the
weather and its only seat was a plank across the
front without even a back to lean on. It was
loaded with two huge barrels, one behind the
other, and a few anonymous cloth-wrapped
bundles tucked in around them. It reeked. Even
in that stinking yard, it reeked.

The boy shrugged. "It's good enough for me,
missee. Run alongside if you prefer."

So that was it! Now Emerald could see the
plan: *If the rack doesn't work use red-hot irons!*
Having failed to subdue her victim with one humiliation, obviously Mother Superior was now
trying something worse. Earth-time people
rarely lost their tempers—they preferred to store
grudges until they found a suitable chance to
take revenge—but Emerald would certainly
have resorted to violence now if the old hag
were present. A handful of stable mire in the
face would be a very promising opening. As she
wasn't there, the only available victim for anger
was this impudent brat. Emerald assumed he
was in on the plot, although he did not *seem* to
be laughing at her. Not yet, anyway. But there

was quite a glint in his eye and he was likely to be better at roughhousing than she could ever be. Discretion prevailed—she restrained her temper.

"What is that appalling stink?"

"Garlic. You must know garlic!"

She did, but this was ridiculous. Those two great hogsheads could hold enough garlic to flavor every meal served in Chivial that year. Who would ever be transporting that amount of garlic around? The stench would be one more torment.

The boy laid one hand on the front wheel and vaulted over it. He grinned down at her triumphantly from the bench. "Coming or not?"

She tried to quell her anger enough to think rationally. He expected her to share that narrow bench with him, and most stable hands had very little idea what a bathtub was for. The garlic should provide some protection, depending on the wind. He was probably richly infested with fleas and lice, too, but after three nights in the cheapest inns of Tyton she must be well inhabited herself. He wasn't scratching too obviously.

If she refused he would drive away and she would be trapped. The Companionship would claim it had paid its debt. It had offered her transportation—who ever promised her padded seats or shelter from the weather? She would be stuck in Tyton with no money, no friends, nowhere to stay, nothing to eat. So she must choose between this whelp and Mother Superior; between his smelly wagon and complete surrender. She wasn't even certain that surrender was still an option. Perhaps she was just being punished out of spite. Furious, she stalked around to the other side, tossed her tiny bundle of possessions aboard, and climbed up beside him.

He smiled innocently at her. "Welcome aboard!"

"What's your name?"

"My friends call me Wart."

"Ug! Then what do your enemies call you?"

"*Sir!*"

He flashed an enormous grin to show that he had thought that up on the spur of the moment. She had to admit that it wasn't bad.

"Then until I know which I am, I'd better call you Sir Wart."

"*No!* I mean, please just call me Wart, mistress."

Why should her feeble joke alarm him so much?

Wart drove through Tyton standing up, so he could see over the horse. He did not speak, being intent on navigating the narrow, crowded streets. Admittedly the clearance was often closer than hairsbreadth, but his clenched teeth and the gleam of sweat on his face suggested that he lacked experience at urban driving. How could he have experience at anything? This was probably the first time his mother had let him go out alone. Once the horse had ambled out through the town gate, though, he sat down and began to whistle. When he wasn't whistling he chattered aimlessly about crops, herds, fine weather, and bad news of Baelish raiders attacking the coast.

Highways in Chivial were rarely more than rutted tracks and often less. The road out of Tyton was much less. The wagon had no springs, and Emerald was going to be thoroughly bruised when she reached Newhurst. That might not be until tomorrow at this pace, but she was in no great hurry to face her mother and admit defeat. Wart's whistling was tuneful and quite pleasant. Horsemen and sometimes coaches went jingling by. The fields were lush, starting to ripen into gold. There was not a cloud in the sky and if the sun had not been shining straight in her eyes—

"Where are you taking me?" she demanded angrily. "We should be going south!"

"You mean we're not?"

She should have noticed sooner. She bared her teeth at the gleam of mockery in his eye.

He laughed. "We'll get to Newhurst, I promise! Just sit back and admire the scenery. I call him Saxon. That isn't his name, but he reminds me of a friend of mine." He cracked his whip

over the horse, whose large rear obscured the
view directly ahead.

Just how foolish had she been? In her stubborn fury she had trusted herself to a boy she
knew nothing about. Highways were so dangerous that stagecoaches carried men-at-arms. Wart
himself seemed like no great threat, but he
might have friends who were. Besides, how far
would the White Sisters go to prevent ex–Sister
Emerald from talking about the sorcery she had
witnessed? Surely they wouldn't hire someone
to cut her throat and leave her body in a ditch
. . . would they?

They came to a toll bridge. Wart chatted for a
while with the tollman—more about weather
and harvests and rumors of another attempt of
the King's life. As he paid up his copper penny,
he said, "This is the road to Valglorious?"

"Aye, lad. Keep on to Three Roads and then
go south."

"Not north?"

"No. North takes you to Farham. Valglorious
is south, past Kysbury."

Wart thanked him and jingled the reins to
start Saxon moving again.

"How long have you had this job?" Emerald
inquired sweetly.

"Ever since I turned thirty," Wart said.

*   *   *

"If you get bored," he suggested an hour or so later, "I'll sing for you. Then you won't be bored. Or at least you won't *complain* of being bored."

"Try me. I'm sure you sing very well."

His juvenile blush burned up on his cheekbones again. "Um . . . truly?"

"I'd like to hear you sing."

Pleased, he cleared his throat and launched into "Marrying My Marion." His voice was a thin tenor, not strong but quite pleasant, although the jolting of the wagon naturally made it unsteady. Even Emerald could not fault his pitch or rhythm so he was probably another time person, like herself. When he reached the chorus she joined in. He shot her a delighted smile and switched to counterpoint and complex trills.

Truth be told, Wart was good company. His quick wit, cheeky humor, and bubbling energy showed that air was his dominant manifest element. His self-confidence puzzled her, although some of it must come from being an adolescent male—she had little experience at judging those. Although air people tended to brag when they were successful and whine excuses when they weren't, Wart seemed content with his world. He chattered, but not about himself. He had been wary when driving in the town, not unsure. The earth-time pairing made her stubborn and patient, but air-time people were usually flighty and impatient. He seemed too relaxed to fit that pattern, either. She would have several days to analyze him, though, as he deigned to explain when they had exhausted the possibilities of marrying off Marion.

"Vincent sent me to deliver a load of hides to Wail and pick up their salt fish. Phew! If you think garlic's bad, you should try sitting on top of that in the hot sun. I dropped the fish off at Undridge and picked up the garlic. He'd told me to stop in at Oakendown and see if they needed any loads delivered—know they're short-handed because of the Monster War, see? Got me and Saxon a free night's board, too. Now we're going to Valglorious. . . ."

However much she might resent being called a load, his tale was believable. She gathered that the duchy of Eastfare owned dozens of estates scattered over half Chivial and ran its own cart-age line, moving specialized produce from one manor to another or to a point of sale. Wart's planned itinerary would take him close to Newhurst in another four days.

"And who gets to keep my fare—you or the Duke?"

"Saxon and I ate it." He wasn't telling actual lies, but he wasn't revealing the whole truth, either. "I eat more than he does, as you'd expect. 'Sides, the Duke's dead, the old one. His son died before he did; his grandson's at court, being a squire. And if Good King Ambrose can teach that brat manners, then he's a better man than I am."

"I don't doubt he is."

He smirked. "Time will tell." Modesty was not one of Wart's burdens.

"So I have to endure four days of this bouncing? And who defends me from highwaymen and brigands?"

"How many highwaymen do you have in mind?"

"Three would be ample." One would be enough.

Wart grinned. "If it's more than three, I run for help. If it's only three, then I kill them myself." He reached behind him and hauled out a sword from under the bench. It was rusty and notched like a saw. Its point had been broken off, but it was a real sword, and she was surprised he had the strength to wave it around so.

"Please! *Don't* bother to brandish it. In fact I'd much rather you put it away before you killed me or the horse."

"You don't trust me!" he moaned, but he slid the weapon back out of sight.

She was starting to trust his motives a little, but she certainly would not trust herself to his arm yet. Give him ten years and he might make a competent defender. Air and time were good elements for a dancer, so they ought to make a nimble swordsman.

* * *

They came to a wide, stagnant-looking river and crossed on a ferry that was no more than a crude log raft. Emerald was glad to climb down and walk around, easing her aches. The ferryman on board was a grizzled, surly man whose job seemed to consist solely of tying up and casting off at the jetties and collecting the fare in between. The real work was done by the boy on the far bank, who led the donkey that turned the windlass that pulled the chains that moved the ferry.

"I'm heading to Valglorious," Wart said. "I turn left at Three Roads, yes?"

The ferryman spat overboard and watched what happened to his spittle before grunting, "No. That'll take you to Farham and Firnesse. Go south."

"South! Thanks."

"Do you think you've got it now?" Emerald inquired.

"See how flat the country is?" he said. "We're in Eastfare—flattest county in Chivial. And the most law-abiding. Vincent's peering over the sheriff's shoulder all the time, so no highwaymen!" He looked to see if she was reassured. "Besides, who'd want to steal two barrels of garlic?"

"It would not be an easy crime to conceal," she agreed. "You're telling me that there's no theft or violence here?" She had seen rows of peasants cutting hay, working their way across the meadows with their scythes and pitchforks, and their women following with sickles to collect what they had missed. She had seen herds of sheep, goats, cattle, and horses. But even in this poverty-stricken landscape, she had seen no houses, because the hamlets and villages all hid behind high stone walls. She said so.

"Ah, I meant *not much*. Remember that we're getting near the sea. Fens and salt marsh and cold gray fog. Where there's sea there's Baels—raiding and slaving, slipping up the creeks in their dragon ships. Even Vincent can't do much about them."

"Who is this Vincent you keep mentioning?"

"Sir Vincent. He was Blade to the Fifth Duke for umpteen years. You know how badly a Blade takes it when his ward dies, but he managed to weather the storm. The old man had named him his grandson's guardian, which probably helped save his reason, so now he runs everything." Wart was clearly enthusiastic about this Vincent. "He's a knight in the Order. Private Blades can only become knights after their wards die. The King summoned him to Grandon to dub him."

This talk of Blades was not out of place. She knew that there was an auxiliary corps of retired Blades who helped out the Companionship by performing odd jobs, although she was vague on the details. Squiring vulnerable ladies on long journeys might well be one such task. She also knew that some of these "Old Blades" had been conscripted into more strenuous duties during the present emergency. Possibly they also supplied boys with wagons as replacements. "Do you often transport Sisters?"

"No," Wart said indignantly, "but I can't afford to be fussy."

Minstrel Boy

THE MORNING AGED AND THE DAY GREW HOT-
ter. Wart asked directions from two shepherds,
one more toll keeper, and the drivers of three
other wagons, always receiving the same answer. Emerald was astonished to discover that
she was enjoying herself. Having never wandered this far from Oakendown since she'd first
entered its gates, she had forgotten how interesting the world was.

"What about you?" Wart asked. "Why are
you not going to Newhurst by coach?"

That was none of his business, but if she lied
to him, he would be entitled to lie to her. She
wasn't very good at lying anyway. "Someone
used some nasty sorcery right in the heart of
Oakendown. I detected it and wouldn't lie about
it, so they threw me out."

"Oh, that's tough! What sort of sorcery?"

The inquisitors of the Dark Chamber claimed
they could detect any spoken lie. Although they

did not brag of it, most White Sisters could do the same, smelling the taint of death on the falsehood. Emerald had enough of the knack to know that Wart had faked his reaction. Sadly she concluded that he was not what he said he was. He was playing Mother Superior's evil games.

"Nasty. I was attacked by a spider bigger than you. I don't honestly know if it was meant to kill me or just frighten me. It certainly did that. No one else will admit it existed at all. I was outvoted."

"Not fair! What do you do now?"

"Find a rich husband."

"Truly?" He had not expected that. He looked at her doubtfully. "Mightn't that be even tougher? Not finding, I mean—I'm sure you won't have to look very long. I mean, finding a husband you want."

"Very likely."

"No parents, brothers?"

"My mother's still alive, but she hasn't got two copper mites to clink together." Either Emerald needed to hear her problem set out in words or else young Wart was just skilled at asking questions, but she found herself telling him all about her father's illness and the enchanters of Gentleholme Sanctuary. "They said they could cure him, but the pain grew worse and worse. Soon he was screaming all the time unless he got a fresh enchantment every day."

Wart's lip curled in horror. "They made his sickness worse?"

"Don't know. Some diseases act that way, so perhaps not. We certainly couldn't prove anything. But they did keep putting their price up."

"This is why the King is trying to suppress the elementaries!" he said indignantly. "His new Court of Conjury is turning up all sorts of horrible cases like that. They have some good sorcerers helping them, and some White Sisters, too. And the Old Blades, of course. You must've heard of Sir Snake, who used to be Deputy Commander of the Royal Guard? He's their leader. . . . Officially they're called the Commissioners of the Court of Conjury—but they're all knights in the Order, so everyone calls them the Old Blades— and they go in and investigate the elementaries. But often the sorcerers fight back with monsters and fireballs and terrible things. They're doing a wonderful job, and—" His baby face colored again. "I'm raving, aren't I?" he muttered. "But you have heard about the White Sisters who help? They're not called the Old Sisters, but . . . Well, you must know."

"I've heard of them." Emerald had volunteered to join them, but so had a hundred others, so she had been turned down. "Some of them have died, also."

"I didn't know that!"

"Why should you?" she asked quietly.

He gulped awkwardly. "Well, I'm interested."

After a moment he sneaked a look at her and evidently decided he had failed to convince. "I met Sir Snake once. You should tell him about this Gentleholme gang."

"I can't prove they made my father's sickness worse. They did put their price up and up until they had taken all our money. When he died there was nothing left." Not even Peachyard, the estate her mother's family had owned for generations.

"Or they let him die when there was nothing left to take?" That was a surprisingly cynical remark. At times Wart sounded much older than he looked. She sensed an unexpected element in his makeup—a faint trumpet note in the far distance, a whiff of familiar scent on the wind. It might be the fading trace of some old magic, perhaps a healing, but somehow she thought it went deeper than that.

"You may be right," she said.

Her brothers had gone off to war and died together in their first campaign. The White Sisters offered almost the only respectable profession open to a woman and would pay even a novice a stipend if she had real promise and the money was needed—as it was in her case. Her mother could no longer see well enough to sew. She could do washing and cleaning, but the rich folk who employed servants had no use for elderly women with twisted hands. She had been living on Emerald's wages. Now it was rich husband or nothing. Trouble was, most rich suitors were old, ugly, crabby. . . .

"If you can detect sorcery," Wart protested, "why can't you get a job doing what White Sisters do? Protecting warehouses from thieves and so on?"

"We don't—I mean *they* don't protect anything. All they can do is warn. Who's going to take my word for what I can do? They'd assume I was in league with a gang of thieves." She smiled at him. "That's enough about me. Let's hear your story." He didn't look old enough to have one.

"Me? I'm a wandering minstrel. Hold this." Thrusting the reins into her hands, he squirmed around to rummage in the cargo. Saxon accepted the change of command without argument, although he twisted his ears nervously when Wart's legs waved in the air. In a few minutes he turned right side up again, clutching a contraption longer than himself.

"Is that a chitarrone?" she exclaimed.

"Almost—an archlute. Very similar. Its mother was a lute and its father an unscrupulous harp."

That described it well. It had the usual catgut strings and a lute's sound box in the normal half-pear shape, in this case beautifully inlaid with brass and mother-of-pearl rosettes. But instead of stopping at the keys, the neck continued for another three feet or more and ended in an-

other set of keys that tuned a second course of
strings—metal ones, running the whole length
of the instrument.

Leaving Emerald to steer Saxon—who was
quite capable of looking after himself—Wart
went to work to tune the monster. That would
have been a hard enough task on level ground.
On a small and bouncing bench, it proved impossible, because the keys for the bass courses
were out of his reach. But he tuned up the standard lute portion well enough and soon his fingers were dancing on it, plucking out torrents
of melody. He played a few pieces, sometimes
singing, sometimes not.

"Wonderful!" Emerald said when he paused
to adjust the keys again. "You are as good as
any minstrel!"

"Better than most."

"You could earn a living with that skill!"

He shook his head pityingly. "There are more
worthy ways a man can earn a living. Any re-
quests?"

She told him to play whatever he wanted.

He stopped at a ford to let the horse drink and
eat from a nose bag. From one of the bundles in
the wagon he produced two meat pies and a
flagon of small beer to share with his passenger.
He played his archlute again, doing much better
on steady ground, but she noticed he was making little use of the extra strings, and when he

did the result was not always tuneful. It was a very beautifully crafted instrument, worth more than he would earn in years.

As their journey resumed, Emerald tried again. "What do you do the rest of the time, when you're not wrestling that lute or following Saxon around?"

He shrugged vaguely. "Odd jobs."

That was a very terse answer from an air person. Sterner measures were called for.

"Who cuts your hair?"

That alarmed him. "What?"

"All the stable boys I ever met looked like pitchforks in hay season. Your clothes are dirty enough and you remembered not to wash your face this morning, but those fingernails? You don't stink and scratch. A skilled barber cut your hair. You don't talk like a hayseed. You're interested in things a hayseed would not be— Sir Snake, for example."

He flushed yet again, this time obviously furious. His anger was directed at himself, though, not her. "I wait on table sometimes. Vincent's very particular about things like fingernails."

He was lying. She just shook her head.

"And I overhear the gentlefolk talking about things like the Old Blades."

"Go tell an owl, boy! You said earlier that you'd met Snake, one of the King's most trusted officers. And 'Vincent'?—you're on first-name terms with a man who runs a county?"

"That has nothing to do with . . . with you."

"Tell me anyway. All of it."

"You wouldn't believe me," Wart said, sounding as if he were trying to talk and keep his teeth clenched at the same time.

"Try me. We have several days to kill."

He sighed. "I ran away from home when I was ten. I had to. My stepfather drank all the time and beat me. He was going to kill me or cripple me. My name was Wat in those days, Wat Hedgebury. I teamed up with a wandering minstrel. He showed me how to strum a lute. Owain was his name, kindest old man you'd ever hope to meet. I sang a bit and passed the hat for him; I learned to do a little juggling and tumbling and carried his bedroll on the road, so I wasn't just charity for him. One day we were performing in Firnesse Castle, which isn't very far from here, and he had a stroke. He died the next day. Baron Grimshank had no use for a minstrel's apprentice—I was ordered to try another county, and soon. On the other hand, he did fancy Owain's lute, which was a good one. Owain had told me I could have it, but no one listened when I said so." Wart grinned ruefully. "I became more than a little cheeky, I'm afraid."

"Not wise?"

"Very foolish. His lordship did not take kindly to being called a thief to his face. He had a henchman called Thrusk, a great hairy brute, big as a bull. They called him the Marshal, but he was just the thug who did the dirty work, grinding the faces of the poor and downtreading peasants. Grimshank told Thrusk to see me off. Thrusk's idea of a fond farewell involved a horsewhip. That left me really mad." Watching her out of the corner of his eye, he added, "So I decided to get my lute back, and that night I broke in."

"You broke into a *castle*?"

"Knew you wouldn't believe me!"

But she did. He had lied earlier and was telling the truth now. Perhaps he was testing her ability to tell the difference. "I didn't say I didn't. I'll decide whether I believe you when I've heard the rest."

That pleased him. He smirked as he said, "It gets stranger. Firnesse Castle sits on the lip of a cliff—not a very high cliff, but high enough and steep enough that they don't bother to post guards on that side. There's no beach, just rocks. Even Baelish raiders could never land a boat there, but at low tide it's no great feat to scramble around the base of the cliff. Climbing up by moonlight was a little trickier." He was bragging, not understanding that it was his dominant element, air, that made him good at climbing.

"Nobody could scale the walls. I didn't have to. Whoever built the castle had put all the latrines on that side—overhanging the drop, upside-down chimneys. It was chilly when the sea wind blew, but the sea did all the shoveling. I was small enough to wriggle up one of the shafts."

"Yucch!"

He scowled at her. "Ever been really hungry? Really, *really* hungry? So hungry you can hardly walk? I had. That lute was *mine* and I needed it to earn a living. I spent *hours* creeping around the Baron's castle hunting for it, terrified I would fall over something or rouse the dogs. When I eventually did locate it, I was too late. The tide had come in and the shore was white with breakers, real killer surf. I hid in a closet until the portcullis was raised at dawn, but they caught me trying to sneak out."

"With the lute, of course?"

"Of course."

And she had thought she was stubborn! "You were ten?"

"Oh, no. Twelve, almost thirteen."

"You were lucky you weren't hanged."

"I very nearly was," Wart said glumly. "Grimshank claimed to be a lord of the high justice and kept a gallows outside his gate to prove it. King Ambrose might argue about his right to use it, but Ambrose wasn't there. After breakfast the Baron held one of the briefest trials ever seen in Chivial and told Thrusk to take me out and string me up. . . ."

For a few moments the wagon rattled on.

Even Saxon twisted his ears around, waiting for
the rest of the story.

"I wonder if that slime pit is still alive?" Wart
muttered, and Emerald heard again that inex-
plicable wrong note, that faint trumpet.

"Baron Grimshank?"

"No, Thrusk. Grimshank was within his
rights—or almost within them. The law says to
hang criminals over the age of ten. But Thrusk
had other ideas. He spoke up to say I was too
young to be hanged. 'Your lordship should
show mercy on a penniless orphan,' he said.
'Why not just send the poor lad back where he
came from?' And Grimshank laughed and told
him to go ahead. That—" Wart thought better
of whatever word he'd been about to use. "That
cur! He was jeering and chortling as he marched
me off to the latrines. He was going to shove me
down a shaft, he explained—*with* my hands tied
and *with* the tide in and breakers all over the
rocks. Headfirst, he said."

He looked at Emerald to see if she was going
to accuse him of lying. She wasn't. Even without
her Oakendown training, she would probably
have believed him. The story was all too horribly credible. Noblemen in remote areas could do
pretty much as they pleased, answering to no
one, and a baron who'd been insulted and made
to look foolish by a friendless juvenile vagabond
could easily react with the sort of brutality Wart
was describing.

"Maybe one day I'll find Thrusk and settle a score or two."

"How did you escape?"

"Just luck, no credit to me. When we got to the latrines, Sir Vincent intervened. He was a guest in the castle, so he shouldn't have meddled. He had no authority at all, except he was a Blade. His beard was gray and there were a dozen of them to one of him, but he didn't even draw his sword. Didn't need to. He told them he and his servant were leaving now and I was going with them—and so was the lute. And that's what happened. That's what it means to be a Blade."

Recalling the two cocksure young men she had briefly seen in Oakendown, Emerald did not doubt that part of the tale either. "They just let him walk out?"

"Yes. If they'd used violence on the Duke of Eastfare's guardian there would have been a hue and cry. He's a member of the White Star, so the King would probably have asked questions. The Lord Chancellor back then was Montpurse, another former Blade. . . . I wasn't worth that sort of trouble to them. Vincent put me on the back of his horse and took me to . . . a safe place."

She caught a whiff of evasion. "What safe place?"

"Valglorious." Wart flashed his most cocky, boyish smile. "So virtue triumphed and I have never been back to see the Big Bad Baron! You believe my story?"

Not that mention of Valglorious. "Some of it," she said, "but not all."

He scowled and silently handed her the reins. He removed his hat, took out his knife. Everyone carried a knife to eat with, and his had seemed quite ordinary—a crude bone handle and a shabby leather sheath. When he drew it, though, she saw that it was a small dagger, with a point and two edges. He soon showed that it was as sharp as a razor, so the blade must be of much better quality than the hilt. Ignoring the bouncing of the wagon, he proceeded to cut his hair, lifting it a lock at a time and slicing it off close to the roots. Pretty soon he had trimmed his whole head to a hideous shaggy stubble.

"How's that?" he demanded, not looking at her.

"Horrible. You look as if you had head lice and your master told the shepherd to shear you."

"Good." He stuffed his hat back on his head. He had slightly protruding ears and now they showed.

"Who are you trying to deceive, if not me?" she demanded.

That question the normally chatty Wart would not answer.

Peculiarer and peculiarer!

Three Roads

THE COUNTRYSIDE DETERIORATED FROM BLACK-soil farmland to a stony plain good only for sheep and goats, apparently uninhabited except for shepherds and their dogs. The only buildings were a few isolated hovels. However, its apparent flatness was deceptive, and it was tufted with patches of gorse and scrub not unlike the new condition of Wart's scalp. Emerald had already noticed that she could rarely see very far in any direction, but she was taken by surprise when a sizable stockade came into view almost as if it had sprung out of the ground.

"Three Roads," Wart announced. "Coaching inn. It's called Three Roads because one road leads from here west to Tyton, one goes north to Farham and Firnesse, and a third runs south to Kysbury and Valglorious."

"I am amazed by the depth of your knowledge."

"We'll spend the night here."

79

"We could cover a league or two more before dark."

"There isn't anywhere to go. Besides, Saxon wants his oats." *Do not argue with the driver!*

He drove the wagon through the gate to a dusty, stony yard surrounded by a variety of thatched buildings—housing, sheds, stables. A mob of ragged boys a little younger than he flocked around him, all yelling for his attention. In such a hubbub Emerald could not make out a word, but Wart obviously knew the proper procedure, for he aimed a finger at one of the largest and said, "You!" The chosen one scrambled aboard, grinning proudly. The rest fell back to wait for another customer.

"Stabling for the night," Wart demanded. "And which road do we take to Valglorious when we leave?"

"Best yer honor park over there under cover," said the guide, pointing with one hand and wiping his nose with the other. "South road goes to Valglorious, if it please you."

"I expect it will whether I'm pleased or not." Wart steered the wagon where he had been directed to park. The boy jumped down to begin unharnessing Saxon. Wart turned a complete somersault in the air before landing on his feet like a cat.

"Oo!" said the boy. "Do that again!" More of the hungry-looking urchins came running over to watch.

"Stand back, then." Wart vaulted up on the wagon again and repeated the feat. Laughing, he refused a third demonstration and turned serious to address the hostler who had appeared to take the guest's orders. "Oats and a good rubdown. Which way to Valglorious?"

"South road," the man said. "You could make Kysbury before dark. Cheaper board than here," he muttered quietly.

"The lady is weary," Wart explained, but he made no offer to play gentleman by helping the weary lady dismount. Instead he rummaged in the wagon for his archlute. Declining offers of help from the grubby boys, he slung it over his shoulder, took up a bundle of personal possessions, and swaggered off in the direction of the hostelry office, leaving his chosen helper guarding the wagon. Emerald followed, assuring the mob of skinny minions that she could carry her own skimpy baggage. She would have hired one of them as porter if she had possessed even a copper mite to pay him.

The door of the main building opened into a sizable timbered hall, dim after the brightness outside. Clattering noises and juicy smells drifted in from a kitchen area at the back, and Emerald guessed that the long tables and benches could probably seat at least two hundred people. Some men were already sitting there quaffing ale, and the big man standing chatting to them was almost certainly the innkeeper. They broke off their argument to scowl at the newcomers.

"Don't need no flea-bitten minstrels here," growled the big one. "And no dancing girls neither."

Wart bristled. He stood the archlute on the floor and said, "Hold this."

"What are you going to do?" Emerald asked nervously. Oakendown did not prepare a girl very well for dealing with men. The world was full of men.

Without answering, Wart strutted forward like a bulldog stalking a bull. He put his fists on his hips and sneered up at the innkeeper, who stood a head taller and twice as wide.

"Are you insulting my companion?"

"You would know that better than me," said the big man.

The ale drinkers chuckled.

"But you do offer hospitality to worthy travelers?"

"Them 'at has money to pay for it."

"Best board for two," Wart said. "Private room for the lady. I'll settle for no more than four in the room, but a bed to myself. A clean blanket. A candle for each of us. Cover and picket for the wagon; oats, water, and a rubdown for my horse."

"Two florins and I'll see the color of your silver now, son."

Not silver—the coin that appeared in Wart's

fingers was gold. He flipped it at the innkeeper, who grabbed but missed it. It rolled under the table, and the big man dived for it as if frightened his customers might beat him to it. While he was down on hands and knees, Wart slapped him on the rump and said, "Good boy!" The ale drinkers guffawed. Emerald was quite certain that Wart had made it happen.

The innkeeper rose red faced and scowling at him with even more suspicion than before, but clearly gold excused anything. He slipped the coin in a pocket and fumbled for change.

"Beg yer pardon, young master. 'Scuse the misunderstanding. I can spare a private room for you also at no extra cost, if that'll make it up to you. Same one the Duke himself prefers when he honors us. Clean linen, of course, always. Best board tonight will be barley mash, roast swan, venison pie, and peaches poached in brandy, if that will be satisfactory, master? All the ale you can drink included. Bread and cheese and small beer to break your fast in the morning if you wish. And her ladyship has only to ask if there is anything at all that my women can do for her comfort." He bowed to her. "Honest Will Hobbs at your service, mistress!"

There was a faint odor of magic about Honest Will Hobbs, but nothing threatening. He probably wore a mild glamour charm to sweeten his customers' view of him.

Wart now looked quite blasé, as if this fawning was only his due. Doubting that she could achieve the same panache, Emerald said as haughtily as she could, "Have you such a thing as a bathtub?"

"Certainly, mistress! I'll have it brought to your room directly, and ample hot water too— no skimping on the hot water, I promise. Softest towels you've ever met, my lady."

"At no extra charge!" Wart said. "By the way, which is the road to Valglorious?"

Emerald's room was cramped and stuffy in the evening heat, but far better than anything she had been granted in Tyton. She enjoyed a long soak to wash off the road dust and ease her bruises. Fresh clothing would have been a joy, but she had nothing to wear except the same drab sack and toe-biting shoes. When she had done the best she could with her appearance, she went downstairs to explore the rest of the inn.

Three Roads was thriving. Four more wagons had arrived and been parked. Like Wart's, each was being guarded by one of the boys. As she watched, a grandiose coach in purple and gold came rattling and jingling into the yard, drawn by four matched chestnut mares. Two liveried grooms stood on the platform at the back and two men-at-arms sat on the roof. The boys swarmed around it like midges and were yelled at by the coachman. She wondered who could afford such an outfit.

On a loading dock outside one of the stable buildings sat Wart, astride a log, strumming his archlute. About a dozen boys were grouped cross-legged around him, singing as he directed. Some adults had drawn close to listen, keeping well back from Wart's hat, which lay invitingly on the edge of this impromptu stage. Emerald wandered over. On solid ground he played much better than he had on the wagon, understandably, although once in a while he still stumbled in the bass. As with an ordinary lute, his left hand had to steady the instrument and also stop the strings while the fingers of his right hand plucked them, but on the archlute he had to pluck the extra bass courses with his right thumb, and this knack he had not quite mastered. He was already better than he had been that morning, though. She wondered again how he had acquired a thing so precious. He had admitted stealing one lute in his brief life.

"Once more right through!" he said, and led his makeshift choir into the ballad again. When they reached the end, the audience clapped. "Take a bow!" Wart said, and the boys jumped up eagerly. "All donations go to the choir, gentlemen, not to me. This minstrel has earned his crust already today." Some men tossed coins into the hat. "Thank you, my lords! May the spirits cherish you all."

His fingers danced over the string. "Now, how many of you know 'Marrying My Marion'?" The show of hands disappointed him. "Suggest something, then." In a moment he had them singing again. He had not known the melody, but he quickly picked it up.

He was a real mystery, was young Wart, and not just because of that faint discordant spiritual element she kept detecting and failing to identify. He went out of his way to draw attention to himself with this public lute playing and by asking every man, bush, and tree the way to Valglorious. He tamed the innkeeper with gold. If he was really the sort of lowly stable hand he was pretending to be, he would never have touched gold in his life. A genuine wagoner would eat in the commons and sleep in his wagon, certainly not in a private bedchamber. Yet he had hacked off all his hair to make himself seem more in character!

Emerald could be sure of only two things. She was certain Wart was in league with Mother Superior, but she enjoyed his company in spite of that. Bother him! Villains were not supposed to be likable.

He wound up the song with a fancy arpeggio, and again a few men threw coppers. "May the spirits favor you, my lords!" He had not been exaggerating about his experience as a minstrel. He was working his audience like a seasoned performer. "This is only our first lesson, you understand, but what better solace than music to ease the cares of a long day? Madrigals and cantatas will have to wait for our second lesson, but if there is any country ballad or simple roundelay that your lordships especially favor, these honest men here will be happy to hazard it for you! Won't you, lads?"

A well-dressed man called for "The Baker's Kittens."

" 'The Baker's Kittens'!" Wart exclaimed. "You all know 'The Baker's Kittens,' my hearties! So let's hear it—'The Baker's Kittens' for two silver florins!" He strummed a few chords, which were almost drowned out by the onlookers' laughter and a howl from the requester that he had never agreed to such a price. It was a good choice, a counting song that anyone could learn as it went along.

The boys had not reached the second kitten before Emerald was distracted by a thin, shrill whistling. Even as she wondered who would be so callous as to spoil a children's singsong like that, she realized that the sound was entirely in her own head. What she was hearing was magic, and the moment she looked around she saw the woman she had encountered at the Acorn in Tyton. She was still some distance away, but the recognition was mutual.

The woman's customary pout twisted into an expression of surprise. She said something to her companion, who offered his arm to lead her over to Emerald. Her voluminous scarlet gown was too heavy for such weather and much too grand for traveling the dusty roads of Chivial. Under a floppy bonnet, her face was shiny with sweat, and her efforts to smile produced a bizarre leer. The steady scream of her amulet was even shriller than Emerald remembered.

"Fancy meeting you here, child! The spirits of chance keep throwing us together! Is this not good fortune?"

That would depend on one's point of view. Plank walls would not keep out magic, so Emerald was in for a wretched night if the innkeeper had assigned this woman a room near hers.

"The pleasure is mine, mistress."

The woman simpered. "Just an hour ago I was telling Doctor Skuldigger your theory that there could be no such thing as a good luck charm. Wasn't I, Doctor? And now see how my amulet has brought us both good fortune!"

"Perhaps it has." Emerald reminded herself that earth people never lost their tempers. That sorcerous racket had nothing to do with luck. She always heard spirits of chance as a thin dry rattle like dead leaves in the wind—or like dice being rolled. She could not guess the purpose of this discordant whistle, only that it twisted every nerve in her body.

"Your lack of faith surprises me." The man had the saddest face she had ever seen, its flesh hanging in folds like a bloodhound's under silver eyebrows. The sword he wore was merely the badge of a gentleman; at his age he would not be expected to use it. His hair was hidden by a wide-brimmed hat, and his expensive, heavily padded doublet and jerkin made his torso seem bulkier than it possibly could be. His spindly shanks could not fill his silken hose, although he stood straight enough. He uttered a sad moaning noise, "Aw? Wherever did you get such a notion?"

None of his business! "From my dear, late grandmother. A White Sister told her so, many years ago."

"Perhaps it was true in her day, but sorcery has made great advances in the last twenty or thirty years." Doctor Skuldigger's voice was as melancholy as his face, a deep groan. "Aw?" he moaned again. "Adepts now can separate the chance elementals, binding the favorable and dispersing the unfavorable." He waited courteously for her to comment. His eyes were bright enough, but the lower lids had sagged to reveal their red lining. Emerald found the effect so repulsive that she had difficulty looking at him.

"I thank you for correcting me, sir. Are you a practitioner of the arts magical?" If he was, then he must be one of the rogues the King had sworn to suppress, because he was talking nonsense. She could not tell whether he was merely ignorant or deliberately lying—the most skilled mother in the Companionship would have had difficulty detecting a death taint under the shrill screech of the woman's spell.

"Aw? Merely a doctor of natural philosophy."

"A scholar of international repute!" said the woman. "I am Mistress Murther."

Emerald curtseyed, as she was expected to. She had still not decided what name she would use in future. "Lucy" she detested. "Emerald Pillow" sounded absurd. And what title could she claim? In her father's day she had been Mistress Lucy of Peachyard. Now she was old enough to style herself Mistress Pillow. Alas, her present threadbare garments would allow her no such grandeur. "I am Emerald, may it please you, mistress."

She was bitterly aware that in the robes of a White Sister she would have outranked both Murther and Skuldigger handily. They would not have dared address her without first sending a servant to ask her permission.

"And what brings you to Three Roads, Emerald?" Mistress Murther inquired as sweetly as could anyone whose mouth was shaped like hers. All the screaming bad temper of their first meeting was now forgotten, apparently.

"I am on my way home."

"Way home to where, Emerald?"

"Newhurst, mistress."

Murther beamed. "Well! Did I not say that our encounter must be good fortune? I happen to be

on my way to Grandon, and Doctor Skuldigger
will accompany me only as far as Kysbury.
Newbury is close by my road. I will let you ride
in my coach, because any company is better than
none. You will enjoy learning how the gentry
travel."

"No!" The unexpectedness of this offer had
sent presentiments of danger prickling all the
way up Emerald's backbone. "I mean, I couldn't
possibly impose on you like that, mistress . . .
very kind . . . other arrangements with my
friends." She had walked into a trap. She was
not sure what sort of trap, but the sensation of
a gate falling behind her was unmistakable.
Snap!

Murther turned away quickly, as if to hide a
smirk of satisfaction. "Come, Doctor. I should
know better than to expect courtesy from the
lower orders." She swept away with her red
skirts brushing the dust and her bejeweled hand
still resting on Skuldigger's arm. The ghastly
sorcerous whistle faded as she moved out of
range.

Emerald stared after her, struggling to understand her own unease. She had refused the offer
too abruptly, but why had that been such a
blunder? For all Murther knew, she was traveling with seven brothers and six grandparents—
for all Murther *should* know, that is. If she had
other information, then she must be another ac-
complice in the obscure Oakendown plot. She

might have seen Emerald on the road, bouncing along in a farmer's wagon with only a boy for company; in that case her poxy chestnut mares ought to have reached Three Roads first, but the spectacular coach had not been parked in the yard when Wart and Emerald arrived.

Just *what* was going on?

Bad News

"THAT ENDS TODAY'S CONCERT, MY LORDS AND ladies." Wart sprang to his feet, archlute and all. The sun was setting, and Honest Will Hobbs would charge for every candle stub. "We thank you for honoring us with your attention, and I do believe that your generosity has provided almost enough to buy every one of these young nightingales a real meal in the commons this evening. From the look of them, it is a treat long overdue. I rashly promised it to them and I shall have to dig deep in my own pouch if the tariff exceeds the take. You, Ginger, take the hat around and see if some—Ah, thank you, mistress! And you, your honor . . ."

As the audience dispersed, Wart turned to Emerald, grinning happily. "Haven't sung for my supper in years! Even if I don't get to eat any of it."

"Why did you bother?" She fell into step beside him as he headed for the main lodging, closely convoyed by the choir. They were anxious to see if he would be true to his word. She was determined to get some truth out of him.

He shrugged. "I suspect Honest Will feeds them the plate scrapings, and not much of those. I've been hungry in my time. Who were your friends?"

She smiled to hide her anger. "I'll tell you when you stop lying to me."

Wart turned to the boy he'd named Ginger and held out a hand to get his hat back. "How much did we make?" He scooped out the coins. "That should do it. Off you go, all of you. Tell Honest Will you're eating at my expense tonight. He knows I'm good for it. You, Freckles, wait a moment." As the rest of the boys vanished in the direction of the kitchens, he said, "What do you know about the lady and gentleman who were talking to Mistress Emerald here a little while ago?"

Freckles looked worried. "Not much, y'r honor. She 'rived in that coach soon after you did. He and 'nother lady came in just after, but their coach left right away."

Wart shot Emerald a cryptic look. "Well, that's a start. Who's the other lady?"

"Just a lady." The boy scratched his tangled mop. "Haven't seen her since she got here."

"Not your fault. I'd guess that for a groat you could find out their names for me, couldn't you? And maybe other stuff too?"

Freckles nodded so eagerly that he almost shook a few off. "Yes, sir, y'r honor! I'll ask. I seen the gentleman around before with the Marshal."

Wart stumbled over a rut and recovered. "Which marshal is that?" His voice had risen half an octave.

"Marshal Thrusk, y'r honor—Baron Grimshank's man from Firnesse." He looked curiously at Wart and muttered, " 'E's a rough sort, y'r honor."

"Yes. Yes, I know he is. So you be careful."

Wart stopped, only a few feet from the door now, and watched as his young spy ran off. He had lost color. Emerald found his pallor strangely worrying. She had assumed that Murther and Skuldigger—if those were their real names—were in league with Wart—if that was his—and thus with Mother Superior. If there were two factions involved, then she had some rethinking to do.

"Thrusk can't hurt you here," she said.

Wart looked at her disbelievingly and licked his lips. "He could, you know! Death and flames! He could ride in here with a dozen men at his back and do anything he liked. Grimshank may be only a baron, not a duke, but who's going to bring his henchmen to justice if one unknown youth dies in a drunken brawl? This is absolutely the worst thing that could have happened, the one thing we—he won't know my name if he hears it," he muttered, as if speaking only to himself. "He might not remember my face—spirits, it's been four years! But the poxy lute will remind him. Flames and death!"

"Four years ago? Getting our stories a little confused, aren't we? You told me you were thirteen then."

"Almost thirteen . . ." Wart's puzzled frown turned into a fierce scowl. "I'm a month older than you are!"

"Oh!" He wasn't lying. Boys matured later than girls, of course, but he certainly didn't look more than a tall twelve or thirteen. *And just how do you know my age, Master Wart?*

"I'm a good guesser. Let's go in and eat while there's still something there to gnaw on."

"No." At the end of a hard day, her resentment boiled over. "You are lying to me now. You have lied to me several times, and you have certainly not told me the whole truth of who you are and why or where you are taking me and who put you up to it. Now I'm going to ask some questions and you are going to answer them, or I shall go straight to Mistress Murther and tell her I shall be delighted to accept her offer of a ride in her coach."

Wart screwed up his eyes for a moment as if resisting a twinge of pain. Then he snarled at her. "No, I will not answer your questions. But you obviously know when I'm lying, so I'll tell you two things. One is that I'm the best protec-

tion you have got or can get, and the other is
that you are in truly terrible danger. So you'd
better just trust me. Now let's go in and eat."

"I'm in danger?" Emerald yelled, "and you
won't tell me why or how or who? That is the
most arrogant, insufferable—"

"It's too late," Wart said miserably. "Telling
you would make the danger much worse, believe me. And if Thrusk and Grimshank turn out
to be involved, that is sheer disaster. Everything
will fall apart."

Good Offer

THE COMMONS HAD BEEN AN ECHOING BARN even when almost empty and would be unbearably noisy any evening, with wagoners and drovers all shouting for service from the overworked staff. Now it had been invaded by thirty skinny, hungry boys, shrilly clamoring for what they regarded as their due—the choir had doubled in size on the way in. Wart pushed his way into the riot to find out who was cheating whom.

Still seething, Emerald headed across to the gentles' dining room where best board was provided. This was a much smaller chamber with a single long table flanked on either side by benches and bearing two glimmering candles to brighten the evening shadows. The dozen or so guests already present were almost all men, and she paused in the doorway while trying to decide whether she should go in or wait for Wart. No doubt delicious odors were wafting from the loaded platters the hurrying servant wenches were delivering, but after a whole day in the wagon she could smell nothing except garlic. The cloying stench of glamours was not a real odor, of course, any more real than the rattling of good luck charms was a real sound. She could detect a faint screech from Mistress Murther's sorcery and see the lady in question sitting alone at the far end. King Ambrose would be having much less trouble suppressing the elementaries if fewer people were deceived by such quackery.

"Aw?" The melancholy noise right at her shoulder made her jump.

"Doctor Skuldigger!"

"Emerald?" Skuldigger attempted to smile at her, although with his spaniel eyes the result was gruesome. "Forgive my prying. My associate, Mistress Murther, is convinced that the reason you shun her is that you can detect sorcery and her good luck charm distresses you."

That was certainly part of it. "I am sorry if I gave offense. I have promised to drop in on an elderly aunt and stay some days with her."

"Aw?" He raised his silvery brows in surprise. "Then you cannot in fact detect sorcery as the White Sisters can?"

Wart's dire warnings rang in her head. "If I were a White Sister, Doctor, then I would not be traveling in my present style."

He sighed. He could not have looked sadder had he witnessed his entire family dying of some terrible disease. "Of course. Your sorrows are your own business and I should not meddle. However, pray grant me a moment to explain. You met Mistress Murther in Oakendown, yes?

"We are anxious to obtain the services of a Sister, and I am sure that you know how much in demand they are these days. We explained that our patron, a most distinguished member of the nobility, is grievously worried that he may be the victim of a curse planted upon him by unscrupulous enemies. Aw? We offered to pay a substantial sum—a very substantial sum, I should add—for a Sister to come and inspect his residence. It may be that there is nothing to this tale and then she would find no hex, aw? But success or failure would not affect the payment of the money." He blinked his droopy eyes at Emerald.

"Do continue, Doctor." She wished Wart would appear. This morbid old man frightened her.

"Alas, the Sisters are grossly overworked nowadays," Skuldigger mourned. "Our mission did not prosper. But if you do have this ability, Emerald, I can promise that a patron such as I have described would offer you the same generous terms as he would a qualified Sister. His house is large, but I assure you that you could visit every corner of it in less than a day. Do not fear that your journey would be unduly delayed."

He did not seem to be lying, but there was too much minor magic in the room for her to be certain of that. She suspected he was hedging his words most carefully.

"Who is this noble patron, Doctor?"

"It would not be advantageous for me to reveal that information at this stage in the proceedings." Skuldigger groaned. "I can, however, promise you that the honorarium he would be willing to pay—for less than two days' effort, I stress—would be at least a thousand crowns."

Emerald gulped. "That is princely!" She and her mother could live comfortably for two years on that.

"Indeed, and I will go further. Should you succeed in uncovering such a hex as I have mentioned concealed upon his premises, a wealthy aristocrat such as he would certainly consider a bonus of an additional thousand as fair reward."

Spirits! With that kind of incentive in the offing, it would take unusual honesty *not* to find a hex or two in the attic.

But . . . *Truly terrible danger* Wart had said, and she knew she must choose between them—the brash boy, who had certainly deceived and entrapped her, and this distinguished gentleman with his so-carefully chosen words. Fortunately Wart appeared at her side then, still wrestling the archlute. Youth and old man eyed each other with equal suspicion.

"I thank you, Doctor," she said, "for your most generous offer. I beg you to allow me time to consider it in the light of my other obligations." She bobbed a curtsey.

Wart offered her his arm—the first gentlemanly gesture she had seen from him. She laid her fingers on it and together they paraded into the dining room.

A Dangerous Thing

THE DECISION COULD NOT BE POSTPONED FOR-
ever. Next morning, when Emerald emerged
from the inn in the mean, clammy light of dawn,
she found the yard in predictable chaos, with
scores of men and boys trying to harness or saddle at least a hundred horses. She had slept
badly, tossing all night, and now was at the end
of the line. She must choose. To remain here at
Three Roads was not an option, unless she
wanted to starve. Lacking a cloak, she shivered
in the chill air.

At the far side of the yard at least a dozen
youngsters were determinedly trying to help
Wart put Saxon between the shafts. They were
getting in one another's way and making the
horse nervous. Closer to hand, Mistress Murther's grooms and coachman were attending to
her team, with her two men-at-arms assisting.
The smelly little wagon and the opulent coach
could not have presented a greater contrast.

Common sense insisted Emerald should grab at Doctor Skuldigger's fantastic offer. Why was she so suspicious? What seemed a great fortune to her might appear trivial to people who could travel in a coach like that one.

She had told Wart about that offer, but he had still refused to reveal any more about himself. She remained convinced that he was somehow in league with Mother Superior. Since she had no idea what Mother Superior was up to, that conclusion was hardly helpful. Most of what he had told her had been true. Murther and Skuldigger's truthfulness she had been unable to judge—which was suspicious in itself. But a thousand crowns was a fortune. It would be salvation to a girl without a penny to her name.

The coach was closer, so she went to it first. There was no sign of Mistress Murther yet, nor the woebegone Doctor, but perhaps she could gather information from the flunkies—exactly who Murther was, for example, and where she lived. It was the sort of vehicle she would expect only the King or maybe a duke to own. It had real glass windows and the body was slung on leather springs to give a smooth ride. A carriage like that one ought to have its owner's arms emblazoned on the doors, but even the men's livery bore no insignia. Very odd! She approached confidently, weaving between horses and men and vehicles, until she was within twenty paces or so of her destination. She stopped suddenly, causing a groom leading a big roan to curse at her and then mutter an apology as he went by.

Magic! Murther's magic or another like it?

Going more cautiously now, Emerald dodged around a couple of wagons and drew nearer. In a few moments she had it worked out. What she was hearing did not come from Mistress Murther lurking inside the coach. It came from the coachman and his helpers, as if all five of them were wearing the same sort of amulet as their mistress. Whatever it was, the magic gave Emerald goose bumps; it would still prevent her from detecting falsehood.

Watching the men, trying to analyze the elements of the spell, she noted that they were a curiously glum lot. Other crews in the yard were talking, joking, even cursing, but Murther's men slouched around in sullen silence. Recalling Mistress Murther's permanent pout, she wondered why this strange sorcery should make its wearers so morose.

She went on past the coach without stopping.

Wart was already sitting on the bench in his wagon. His smile seemed genuine—and welcome. "Good chance, Emerald!" He had to shout over the racket as a four-horse dray loaded with lumber went clattering past, heading for the gate. "Have you made your decision?"

"Wart, I need the money!"

His face fell. "Don't believe in the money.

Skuldigger is known to consort with Thrusk, Grimshank's man, and you know what I think of those two. I can't find out any more about Mistress Murther. Anyone rich enough to drive that carriage ought to be armigerous—and if you look very closely at the door, you can see that it used to bear a device, but it's been painted over. I could make out a swan and two badgers and those are not Grimshank's arms. It may mean only that Murther has just bought the vehicle. The boys haven't seen it around here before." He shrugged. "Or her. And the other woman seems to have disappeared altogether, but Skuldigger certainly arrived with another woman. Emerald, I'm sure your friends are up to mischief."

"I'm sure you are!"

His boyish face colored. "If you go with them, you may be heading into terrible danger."

"And if I stay with you I will not?"

"I told you that you were safer with me. I repeat that: *You are safer with me!* Am I telling the truth?"

Safer, not safe. She nodded, trying to keep her teeth from chattering. The sun was touching the roof ridges, so the world would warm soon. The sky was a glorious blue already. Saxon rattled his harness and stamped his great hooves, anxious to be gone.

"Wart, you're telling me what you think is the truth, but that doesn't mean it's necessarily right. Whoever's behind you may have lied to you." Mother Superior had lied to her.

Wart opened his mouth to protest and then shut it with a click. That was a bad sign—he was more or less admitting the truth of what she had just said. "What do you want?"

"The whole story."

He shook his head. "I swore I wouldn't tell you. And if you're right, I may not even know the whole story. I'm sure I don't."

"Then I will take my chances with Doctor Skuldigger and Mistress Murther." She turned away. She was bluffing, because being shut up in the carriage with all that shrieking sorcery would be unbearable torture.

But Wart didn't know that. "Emerald! Come back!" He showed his teeth angrily. "I'll bend my promise this far. I will tell you *why* we're doing this and *why* it matters and *why* I can't tell you any more than that." He pulled a face. "I shouldn't! I don't like the situation any better than you do and I'm in much worse danger than you are. I almost hope you will run away from me, because then I'll be safe. Safer than I am now, anyway."

Burn him, he was still telling the truth! Emerald tossed her bundle into the wagon and lifted the edge of her skirt to climb over the wheel.

*   *   *

He turned Saxon out the gate onto the sunlit trail, but he had barely cleared the corner of the stockade before a shrill voice shouted, "Wart!" The boy he called Freckles came running.

Wart reined in Saxon, although with some difficulty, for the horse was frisky and eager. "What's the tumult, m'hearty?"

"The Doctor promised me a whole penny if I'd keep watch and see which road you took!"

Wart laughed and reached in his pouch. "Then this is your lucky day. Here's another for telling me you're going to tell him." A coin spun through the air.

"You want me to tell him wrong?"

"No. Tell him the truth. Be the good little boy your mother would be proud of."

Freckles curled his lip in disgust at this insult and examined his new treasure. "Me mom says telling truth is stupid and gets you in trouble."

"Go back and tell her she's wrong this time."

"Dunno know where she is."

"Then keep it a secret. I suspect the nasty Doctor will have more than one spy watching me, so you won't get your money from him if you tell him lies. And don't forget how I said you could earn a silver groat." He thumped the reins down on Saxon's back and the wagon rattled forward on the south road. "Beautiful morning!"

"Speak!" Emerald said menacingly.

"I hear and obey, Your Grace. Don't you

know that a little knowledge is a *dangerous thing?*''

"I'll risk it."

He shrugged. "Don't say I didn't warn you. We are serving the King's Majesty. You did not volunteer for what you are doing, but you will be well rewarded at the end of it. If you die, then your family will be compensated. Will that satisfy you?"

It ought to surprise her. Curiously, it did not. One of the few conclusions that she had reached in the night was that young Wart talked a lot about the King's Blades and claimed to know at least two of them. If someone other than—or as well as—Mother Superior had put him up to this escapade, one of those men was probably the culprit. "No."

"You are safer not knowing."

"I don't care. You promised."

He sighed. "You've heard about the Night of Dogs. There have been other attempts on the King's life since then."

"Three, I heard."

"More than that." The wagon was leaping and bouncing as Saxon raced along the road, feeling his oats from the previous night. He would soon tire and slow down to his usual amble, but in the meantime his passengers might be beaten to pulp. "That's a state secret and I am telling you the truth. Do you still want me to go on?"

State secrets could be dangerous things to know. They were not normally passed on by juvenile stable hands. "Yes."

Wart sighed. "Are all girls so stubborn?"

"Are all boys so secretive?"

"Probably not. You must know this better than I do, but I'm told that not all White Sisters sniff magic quite the same way—that the same spell may seem different to different Sisters. Is that right?"

"Yes. It's very personal. What seems a scent to one may be a sound to another, or a cold feeling, or almost anything."

He nodded. "Lately the attacks have been getting more subtle. Two weeks ago someone slipped a poisoned shirt or something into the royal laundry basket. The White Sisters detected it and the whole batch was burned, but it's a safe guess that the purpose was to kill the King." Wart shot her a wry glance, as well as he could while the wagon was bouncing so hard. "I trust you are a loyal subject of His Majesty?"

"Of course!" If such an evil could be smuggled into the palace, then the spider monster she had seen in Oakendown was not so surprising after all.

A coach went rattling past them, but not Murther's coach. It vanished southward in a cloud of dust. Then two horsemen . . . Last night's residents at Three Roads were scattering to the four

winds. Three winds, actually, as little but sea
and salt marsh lay to the east.

"The problem is," Wart said grimly, "that the
magic got past two Sisters without being noticed
and almost past a third. A similar booby trap
turned up in the royal stables a few days later,
and that one was even harder to detect—had it
not been for the laundry warning they would
almost certainly have overlooked it."

"This is nonsense you are talking."

"Oh? I'm lying?"

"No, but you have been misinformed. If the
sorcery was powerful enough to do real harm,
that is. If all it was designed to do was produce
a faint itch, say, or a bad smell, well, then it
might slip by. But a White Sister should recognize anything fatal at least twenty paces away.
Easily!"

"Saxon, you idiot! Slow down!" Wart rose to
peer over the horse, then sat down again, as
much as bouncing could be classified as sitting.
"Yes, that's what I was always told—anything
powerful enough to worry about will show up
to the sniffers like a dead pig in a bed. But that
isn't true anymore! Whoever the conspirators
are, they're managing to mask one magic with
another, a magic-invisibility spell, you could call
it."

"Rubbish!" she protested. If what he said was
true, then the entire Companionship of the

White Sisters might find itself useless! "It can't be done."

"Why not?"

"Because the second magic—the magic wrapping, call it—would be detectable also, so you'd need to put another layer around that one and then another. . . ." But was that necessarily so? The wrapping itself need not be a major sorcery, just a deception spell, and if the elements could be properly balanced, perhaps it would not show up very much at all. She had never heard such a thing mentioned in Oakendown, but even the possibility might be a forbidden topic, best never discussed. "Maybe it could be done," she admitted, "but it would be very difficult. It would need a team of very skilled sorcerers and . . ."

"And?" Wart waited for her to finish the thought.

"Oh no!" Horrors! "And a White Sister?" The novices and postulants at Oakendown were kept well away from magic until they became attuned to the natural flow of the elements. Sorcerers could never develop the same abilities because they were constantly in communion with spirits. The two crafts were direct opposites.

Wart sighed. "More than one. At least two, but the more the better. Suppose you want to kill the King and you devise a booby trap—a petition, for example, a roll of parchment, or a fishing rod, something he will handle in person. Suppose you then cloak its magic in a magic wrapping. You might find that the package would deceive two Sisters, yet still be detected by a third. Grand Wizard of the Royal College of Conjurers says that there must be at least two Sisters working with the conspirators, and he would guess four or five."

She could find no flaw in the logic. Sorcerers trying devise a magic wrapping would be like blind people trying to paint a picture. Only White Sisters could tell them how effective their work was, or how it should be improved.

"But we all take vows not to use our skills for evil purposes or for our own enrichment. *They* do, I mean."

Wart let the wagon rattle on—a little slower now—for several minutes before he spoke. He twisted around to stare back past the barrels. With the sun low in the east, the scrubby landscape was more obviously rolling than it had seemed the night before. A solitary flock of sheep grazed off to the west. Three Roads was no longer in sight.

"Renegade Sisters?" he said at last. "I didn't say they were cooperating willingly, although we think at least one of them must be."

"I refuse to believe *any* White—"

"We know of one who was kidnapped right out of her house. A former Sister, married, had a young baby. The baby went with her. I think she could be made to cooperate, don't you?"

Emerald shivered as if the day had suddenly turned cold again. "Would they really do that?"

"They're traitors!" Wart yelled. "They're trying to kill their king—and if they're caught, they will be hanged, drawn, and quartered!" He lowered his voice again. "They're evil enough and desperate enough to do anything you can imagine and a lot of things you can't. *That* is why I mustn't tell you any more. *That* is why I have already told you far too much."

"I don't see—" Suddenly she did see. It was like a shutter being thrown open to let daylight into a cellar. *"Bait?* Spirits! You set me up as *bait*!"

Wart muttered, "Oh, vomit!" under his breath.

"Arrogance!" she said. "Cold-blooded arrogance! You worked out that if the conspirators' masking spells are good enough to fool their own White Sisters but not all the Sisters at the palace, then what they need is more Sisters to help them. And the best place to find White Sisters is Oakendown, so you guessed that they would be snooping around there. *Snake!*" she shouted. "Sir Snake! You mentioned that you'd met him, but you made it sound like a long time ago. I bet the last time you saw *Sir* Snake wasn't any longer ago than the day you met me or the day before—was it?"

Wart stared straight ahead, not speaking. His

face looked ready to burst into flames.

"And you got Mother Superior to—No, *Sir Snake* got Mother Superior to expel me! That was the only reason for the spider, wasn't it? You provided a sorcerer to create that spider and frighten me and six children out of their wits. I was trapped, wasn't I? Used! You had me thrown out with no money. Shamed, humiliated. You left me hanging around the gatehouse for days, hoping the traitors would be on the lookout for vulnerable White Sisters. I suppose you even spread rumors of my disgrace around town." She was so indignant she could hardly speak. *"Bait!* You used me as bait!"

Wart glanced at her miserably. "It wasn't my idea."

"But you helped. You're guilty too. You sold your soul to that precious Sir Snake and his Old Blades." Mother Superior was another and must have been helped in the deception by a fair number of senior Sisters. "How much did they pay you? Just the archlute? Is that your reward? And that gold you were flashing around so freely at the inn, I expect. I hope you enjoy your ill-gotten wealth, because it would choke me if I'd earned a penny than way. So Murther and Skuldigger are the first nibble? What happens now? If I'm the bait, then where's the hook?"

Wart stood up to peer over the horse and then look back over the barrels.

"Speak up!" Emerald shouted. "You've told

me enough that you can't stop now. I don't have a baby to protect. I know not to try and lie to a White Sister—if they do have traitor Sisters on their team, which I don't believe. Tell me. I'll keep quiet."

Wart looked down at her. "Keep quiet? Will you keep quiet if they nail your hand to a bench and start cracking your fingers with a hammer?"

She shuddered. "I'll think of you when they do it. Come on! You wouldn't just trail bait without a net or a hook of some kind." Magic? No, if Wart had any magic up his sleeve she would have detected it right away. "Tell me! What happens now?"

"What happens now," Wart said harshly, "is that the armed men up ahead stop us and keep us there until the coach coming behind us arrives. Then you get carried off, I expect. You're valuable. You're what they want. If you behave yourself you should be all right, at least for a while. I'm no use to anyone, so the odds are that I get my throat cut. That's what happens now."

Ambush

IT WAS A BEAUTIFUL SITE FOR AN AMBUSH. THE trail ran along a very gentle ridge, a stony swell on the landscape; and the dips on either hand were marshy, with reeds and bulrushes. Saxon could not haul the wagon across a swamp, no matter how narrow. Furthermore, the next ridge to the east was slightly higher and the one to the west bore a mane of thorny scrub along its crest, so the site was hidden from any distant onlookers. Perfect.

Wart hauled on the reins; the wagon rattled to a halt.

About a hundred paces ahead, a line of men-at-arms blocked the road. Five of them were busily moving their arms as if working a pump or a bellows, but Emerald realized that they were actually winding up crossbows, the bows standing upright in front of them, each steadied by a stirrup. Another man in the background held the horses. The seventh was obviously the leader, standing on the verge with folded arms.

About the same distance to the north—back the way they had come—a large coach was approaching. The trap was closed.

The bowmen finished spanning their bows and lifted them to the horizontal. On the leader's command, each one pulled a steel-tipped quarrel from his quiver and laid it in the firing groove. The sight of loaded weapons pointed at her made Emerald's skin try to crawl right off her.

"What's the range of those things?"

"Farther than us, but they're only accurate close up." Wart's voice sounded very thin. His blush had totally gone now. He was pale to the lips.

Another command and the men raised their bows, laying the stocks against their cheeks, ready to shoot. They wore swords, steel breastplates, helmets shaped like hats with wide brims. They began to advance in line abreast, and Emerald could not help but imagine one of them stumbling in a rut and accidentally pulling the trigger of his bow. Their leader swaggered close behind, staying out of their line of fire. His red cloak was bright and grand; his helmet was more elaborate than theirs, with cheek pieces and a flange covering the back of his neck. He was a very large man, bushily bearded, armed with only a sword and dagger.

"Thrusk," Wart said hoarsely. He turned and reached under the bench.

"Oh, no!" Emerald muttered. Then she saw that Wart had found the sword and repeated, much louder, *"No!"*

He was staring at the advancing enemy with hate in his eyes and teeth bared like a dog. At least he had enough sense to hold the sword out of sight behind him—so far.

"Wart, you're crazy! Throw it away right now! *Now*, before they get here. You show that thing and they'll put five bolts through you in an instant." Her protest produced no result at all, as if he had become completely deaf. *Men! Why did men always think violence could solve anything?* "Wart, please! They're in armor—you're not! Even if they didn't have bows, they're trained men-at-arms! You wouldn't have a hope against one of them, let alone six!" She could hear the coach in the distance behind her, coming slowly. Thrusk and his bowmen were going to arrive first.

"Run, Wart! Leave me and the wagon. Just run! See those bushes up—"

"Run? Run from bowmen? Run from horsemen?" He did not add, *Run through a swamp?* as he might have done.

"At least throw that wretched old sword away. Be polite, don't annoy them, then maybe Thrusk won't remember you, maybe they'll just leave you here and take me. And I'll be all right—you said so yourself. Then you can go and . . . and . . ."

It wasn't working. Wart still snarled, never taking his eyes off his old enemy approaching. "*Now* do you see why I didn't want to tell you? *Now* do you understand why I was strictly ordered *not* to tell you anything *at all?* If you breathe one word, one hint that you were staked out for them to find, then we're both cold meat."

"Yes, Wart. I'm sorry I didn't trust you."

"At least you have a chance."

"So do you, if you'll just throw away that sword. Now, please let go of it and get down from the wagon. *Don't* make them see you as a threat, Wart! Be humble, Wart, please." She had a sudden clear image of him sitting there nailed to the garlic barrel by a bolt through his head. And the shot might hit her by mistake.

"As far as Thrusk is concerned, I'm already under sentence of death." His voice had dropped to a growl.

She had never seen real hate on a man's face before—she could no longer think of Wart as a boy when he looked like that. Yet his only hope of survival lay in seeming harmless to the brigands.

The shrill wailing of that awful sorcery was back, but it was coming from the Marshal and his men—all of them, as far as she could tell.

"Halt!" Thrusk barked.

His little troop halted. They were only a few

feet in front of Saxon's nose now—two on the left and three on the right, placed to shoot past the horse at the passengers. The squeaks and hoofbeats in the rear died away as the coach stopped. Horses whinnied greetings. Emerald risked a glance behind her and was not at all surprised to see Murther's purple monster and its four beautiful chestnuts. One of the grooms was opening the door and pulling down the steps, and the armed guards were clambering down from the rooftop seat. Wart with his rusty sword was seriously outnumbered.

Thrusk walked along the verge, staying clear of his men's line of fire, on Wart's side of the wagon. "Get down, both of you."

As Emerald began to move, Wart said, "Stay where you are! By what right do you contest our passage on the King's highway, fat man?"

Thrusk showed yellow teeth in his black jungle of beard. "By right of might, shrimp. Now get down or I'll have my men—Huh?" He took one step closer, peering harder at Wart. So tall was he and so low the wagon that he was looking down, rather than up. "By the eight! It's the minstrel brat, the sneak thief! Well, well, well!" His roar of laughter sent avalanches of ice down Emerald's backbone.

Wart glanced back. So did Emerald.

And so did Thrusk.

Doctor Skuldigger was just emerging from the coach.

Taking advantage of that momentary distraction, Wart made a flying leap from the wagon, swinging the rusty sword in a murderous slash. What he might have achieved with it against a man wearing breastplate and helmet was never established, because he caught a toe on the wheel. His war cry became a howl of despair and he pitched headlong, sprawling in the dirt like a wagonload of firewood. He rolled and his sword rattled away across the gravel.

Emerald ducked, but no crossbow bolts flashed through the air.

"Flames!" Thrusk roared. "Try to kill me, would you?" He grabbed the front of Wart's jerkin and hoisted him up bodily with one hand, as if he weighed no more than a blanket.

Wart sagged in his grasp like a rag doll, half stunned by his fall, eyes wobbling, but evidently undaunted. "Killing's too good for you, stinkard!"

Thrusk roared in fury and slammed a fist the size of a loaf of bread against Wart's jaw.

Emerald screamed at such brutality. Wart hit the ground again, flat on his back. But Thrusk then drew his sword as if to chop off his opponent's head and the time for screaming was past. *"Leave him alone!"* She was down on the road between the two of them with no clear recollection of hitching up her skirts and completing the sort of mad leap that Wart had attempted, even in her ill-fitting shoes. "You get back!" she yelled, spreading her arms.

Thrusk snarled and drew back his free hand to swat her aside. An instant before he would have spread her as flat as he had spread Wart, a sepulchral voice spoke at her back.

"Stop!"

At that soft moan, the giant froze.

"Incompetent oaf!" Doctor Skuldigger came mincing forward, followed a few paces behind by Mistress Murther and another woman. "Aw? What are you doing, Marshal? Tell your men to unload those bows at once."

Thrusk barked an order at his troop. "This trash tried to kill me." He gestured with his sword at the unconscious Wart, the move being close enough to Emerald's knee that she jumped aside. His attitude to the Doctor was one of sulky deference.

Skuldigger was in charge. He sighed. "Aw? I instructed you that there was to be no bloodshed."

Blood was still being shed. Emerald knelt to examine Wart. He was out cold and bleeding badly from the mouth. Whether he had lost teeth or simply split his lips she could not tell, but his jaw was swelling up like a red cabbage. Perhaps this experience would cure some of his tricky habits. Having seen him do midair somersaults off the wagon, she could not believe he could fall flat on his face like that. He must have been faking, although she could not guess why.

"Doctor!" she shouted. "This man has been injured and needs attention."

"I know that brat of old," Thrusk growled. "He's a felon! He was sentenced to hang years ago. Now he tried to kill me. Let me have him, master, and—"

The Doctor moaned. "Must I always be served by idiots? He is half your size, ninny."

The giant growled defiantly. "He attacked me with a sword. You told us we could defend ourselves."

"Bah! He could not hurt you if you had both hands tied behind your back." Skuldigger seemed moved close to tears. He turned to the two women. "Well?"

Murther stayed silent, regarding the world with her inevitable pout. The other woman was younger and might have been judged beautiful if she had made an effort to dress better, comb her hair, stand up straight. Her gown and cloak had originally been of good quality but looked old and abused, as if handed down from a mistress to a servant. She herself was strangely hunched, arms tightly folded across her breast like someone freezing, although the day was warming rapidly. She might be seriously ill. She shook her head and mumbled something Emerald did not catch.

"Stand back!" Skuldigger commanded. "Go, Murther!"

"Back to the horses!" Thrusk roared. He

marched off with his bowmen. Mistress Murther stalked back to the coach with her nose in the air. The sorcerous whistling faded almost to nothing.

"Well?" the Doctor demanded again.

The woman looked Emerald over without ever meeting her eyes. She gazed down at Wart, then shuffled over to lay a hand on the wagon. "Nothing," she muttered.

Skuldigger moaned. "You are quite sure of that, Sister? You do remember that any carelessness on your part will have terrible consequences?"

For a moment fire glinted in her eyes, and she bared her teeth at him in fury or hatred. Then the former hopelessness fell over her face like a veil. "Yes, Doctor, I remember."

For a moment the horrible old man seemed almost about to smile. "Then you do not need to worry about being rescued, do you? Sir Snake has outsmarted himself again. Go back to the carriage."

She obeyed, shuffling away as if she carried all the sorrows of the world on her shoulders. Thrusk returned.

Skuldigger sighed heavily, scowling down at the unconscious Wart. "Your mindless brutality has put a serious hitch in my plans. This boy cannot ride, and I will not have him bleeding all over my coach."

"Tie him across a saddle," Thrusk suggested.

"And if we are seen, idiot?"

"He was condemned to hang years ago, little vermin. Let me hang him, or chop his head off, master. Please?"

Skuldigger sighed mournfully. "No, he will be of use in our experiments. Here is what we shall do. Bring him in the wagon. Lay him face-down so he does not choke on his own blood, aw? You will escort us to the turnoff and wait there for the wagon, as previously planned. If you are quite sure that there is no pursuit, you will bring the boy to the boat."

"And if there is?" the Marshal demanded, his eyes narrowing to shadowed slits inside his helmet.

"I already ordered you to slay as many of them as you can, did I not? But in that case you may kill the boy first. Will that satisfy your blood lust, brute?"

"If I have time to do it properly."

"And see there is not one spot of blood left on the road here—you understand?"

"Yes, master. Not a drop."

"Now we must hurry or we shall miss the tide." The old man turned his agonized, droopy eyes on Emerald. "Give me your bonnet."

"I certainly will not! And I'll thank you to explain by what right you behave like a common brigand on the King's—"

"Hit her."

Thrusk raised a huge fist.

"No!" Emerald cried, stumbling back.

"If you are hurt," the Doctor moaned, "you will have only yourself to blame. Now, the bonnet."

Emerald hauled off her bonnet without ever taking her gaze away from the leering Thrusk; she handed it to the Doctor.

"Now get in the carriage."

"I will not! Are these highwaymen yours, Doctor, because—"

She did not see Thrusk move. One minute he was two paces away from her and the next he was standing over her, chuckling, and she was flat in the dirt. Her head rang. The shock of it left her gasping like a landed fish.

"Aw? I said, 'Get in the carriage.' Now you will force me to have the Marshal kick you in the ribs until you obey. One . . ."

Emerald scrambled giddily to her feet and lurched along the road to the coach. She might not know for certain who headed the conspiracy against the King, but she could name a convincing suspect. The other woman was obviously the kidnapped Sister whom Wart had mentioned, the one whose child had been taken hostage. Now Emerald was in the same boat. The bait had been taken, but where was the hook?

Knights to Remember

STALWART WAS NEVER AWARE OF RECOVERING consciousness. He just gradually understood that he was in a lot of pain and helpless to do anything about it. For one thing he was face-down in a very smelly box, being bounced up and down on bare boards; he could see nothing except chinks of daylight between them. For an-other, he was bound hand and foot with a noose around his neck, so he dared not try to sit up in case it would choke him and he would not be able to loosen it again. The rope around his wrists was so tight that he could feel nothing at all in his hands. If the blood supply was cut off too long they would die and rot. What use was a swordsman with no hands?

His mouth and jaw felt as if Saxon had kicked him there with all four shoes at once; some of his teeth were loose on that side and the taste of old blood was nauseating. To make it worse, his mouth was held open by a gag, a rag tied around his head. Guess who had done that—no prize offered? He could hear hooves and sometimes two voices, although he could not make out what was being said. The strings of the archlute murmured somewhere close to his ear. Under a heap of smelly sacks he was sweltering, but even in this poorly inhabited part of Chivial, no one could drive around with a corpse in plain view and not get asked questions.

So he was alive, when he had not really expected to be. That situation did not seem much of an advantage at the moment, and Thrusk would make sure it did not last long.

Someone cleverer than Thrusk was in charge, though.

"We mustn't let the enemy suspect that the wagon is being followed," Snake had said. "So we'll stay well back. One of us may ride forward and pass you from time to time, but don't react. Don't show you recognize us. Talk to people whenever you get the chance, because we'll ask the ferrymen and other locals if they remember seeing you going past."

It was a good plan, but someone had been smart enough to see through it. Now the wagon was still trundling along the highway and it still had a man and a woman on the bench. It might be a long time before the Old Blades realized that a switch had been made and Emerald was gone.

Stalwart had known right from the moment

Bandit swore him into the Guard that he was destined for danger, and Snake had spelled it out for him an hour or so after that. He had known it but never really believed it—not like he believed now. That morning the prospect of adventure had blinded him to everything else.

He left Ironhall in public shame, head down to avoid the disbelieving stares of the few juniors who happened to be around. There were no seniors in sight—thanks to Bandit and Grand Master, probably—but Bandit himself was at the gate, talking with the Blades guarding it. He did not even look around as Stalwart slunk past, but some of the others scowled and made biting remarks about quitters and cowards. It was not a happy moment.

As soon as he was off by himself amid the lonely wilds of Starkmoor, his usual cheerful spirits returned. Hope and adventure put a spring in his stride and the wind danced with his cloak. He raced along the dusty track, jogging and walking by turns, bothered little by the weight of the lute on his back and not much more by the hunger in his belly. He never did reach Broom Tarn. About half an hour up the road he turned off on the shortcut over the Rockheap; on the far side of that, safely out of sight of Ironhall, two saddled horses grazed the wiry moorland grass. The man lying on his back nearby seemed intent on the hawks circling in

the blue heavens, but he must have been keeping a eye on the horses, too. When Wart came
in sight they raised their heads and he sprang
up.

He came striding over, hand out in welcome.
His clothes were nondescript, almost shabby,
but the sword at his side bore a cat's-eye on the
pommel. He was not only a Blade, he was the
one Stalwart had been desperately hoping he
would be, Sir Snake himself—Deputy Commander of the Guard during Stalwart's first
years at Ironhall, later dubbed knight and released, then called back to lead the volunteer
group they called "the Old Blades." The name
he had chosen long ago still fitted him, for he
was exceedingly lean; he had a knife-blade nose
and a thin mustache. He was devious, they said,
clever as a forestful of foxes. He had not named
his sword anything obvious like *Fang* or *Venom*.
No, she was called *Stealth*, and that said a lot
about him.

His eyes twinkled as he pumped Wart's hand
and thumped his shoulder.

"Was counting on you," he said. "Never
thought you'd fail us. Welcome to the Blades,
brother!" He laughed, joyous as the summer
morning. "And welcome, O Youngest of All
Blades, to the *Old* Blades, the unbound Blades!
I have a job for you that will make your hair
stand on end!" He made that sound like a great
virtue. He led the way over to the horses—and

what horses they were! The King himself rode nothing better.

"I brought a sword for you to wear. Not a cat's-eye, I'm afraid, but we'll get your real sword to you shortly. Can't have a Blade walking around unarmed, like a peasant."

"That's very kind of you, Sir Snake."

"Oh, you go pile *that* manure elsewhere, my lad! You're one of us now. You call me 'Snake' or 'brother,' understand? There's food in the saddlebags and you can eat as we ride. . . . The King is 'sire' to his face and 'Fat Man' when he's not around. Bandit is 'Leader.' You can be polite to Dreadnought and Grand Master when you feel like it, but don't ever give me titles. Now let's—" He paused for an instant. "And Durendal. Him we honor because he's still the greatest of us all. No one else. Now get your tender young behind on that saddle. We have the width of Chivial to ride before we'll see a bed tonight. Yes, I'll tell you all about it as we go." He went to put his foot back in his stirrup and then paused again. "I'm told they call you Wart. Which do you want to be from now on— Wart or Stalwart?"

"Wart's more fitting . . . Snake. Call me Stalwart when I grow into it."

The glittery eyes studied him for a moment. "You may have earned it by next week."

"Then call me Stalwart next week," the boy said crossly, and swung himself up into the saddle. He wished they would all stop talking about danger and tell him what it was they wanted him to do.

If they did not ride the whole width of Chivial that day, they certainly crossed most of it, thundering along on the finest horses Stalwart had ever ridden. Until that journey he had rather fancied his skills in the saddle, but Snake was superb. Every hour or so they had changed mounts at a posting inn, taking horses reserved for the Royal Couriers, the best steeds in the land. As they rode, Snake spelled out the plan.

"It's risky, of course," he admitted, "but I think we've thought of most things that can go wrong." He had not foreseen Thrusk.

Stalwart had blundered, yes. He had thrown his expense money around at Three Roads. That had been a stupid childish impulse, exactly the sort of mistake that might warn an enemy he was not what he was pretending to be. Nor should he have told Emerald that she was being used as bait. Yet he might still have pulled it off if Thrusk had not come on the scene. Thrusk's involvement had been the worst of all possible luck, misfortune that could never have been predicted.

He remembered how Thrusk had sworn to get even with him, that day at Firnesse Castle.

*   *   *

On the way to the latrines, Thrusk had collected a dozen men to come and watch the fun. Public executions were always a big draw, and no one had ever seen a thief executed quite this way before. The jokes were flying thick and fast.

When they reached their destination, one man blocked their path. He had gray in his beard and weather lines etched in his face, but a cat's-eye shone yellow on the pommel of his sword, and a diamond Star on his jerkin warned that he was in royal favor.

"This joke is not funny, Marshal," Sir Vincent said quietly. "Untie the boy. I'm taking him off your hands."

Thrusk responded with a drum roll of oaths. Vincent took hold of his sword hilt and there was silence.

"If you call me one more bad name I shall draw. If you force me to draw, for any reason whatsoever, then you die first. This I swear."

That was all it took. That was what it meant to be a Blade, even a Blade with a grizzled beard facing a dozen young men-at-arms. Thrusk sent a page to tell the Baron what was happening. He came at once and followed them all the way to the gate, screaming outrage. "Arrest that man! I am a lord of the high justice! This is rebellion against the King's Peace! I shall complain to the Privy Council!" On and on. He was a plump little man with absurdly bowed legs and a very shrill voice. Sir Vincent mostly ignored him, and nobody dared interfere with Sir Vincent.

Unable to believe this change in his fortunes, little Wat Hedgebury the minstrel's apprentice walked out under the portcullis clutching the lute he had almost died for—in hands that would not stop trembling. Vincent's servant was waiting there with two horses. The knight gave the man the lute to bring and pulled the boy up behind him on his own mount, although he still stank mightily of his climb up the sewer in the night.

Before Vincent could urge his mount forward, Thrusk's voice bellowed down from the battlements: "Don't think you're going to get away with this, thief! You can't hide behind that old brigand forever. One day I'll catch you and give you what you deserve."

Vincent turned his horse to get a better view. "You want to come down here and repeat that?"

"Go while you can, old man. We're about to loose the dogs on you. And if you do take that trash with you, don't be surprised when your silverware starts disappearing. One day we'll stretch his neck for him."

"Don't be so sure of that!" Vincent roared, the first time he had raised his voice. "Boys grow up. Next time you meet it may be his turn to jeer." He kicked in his heels and the two horses cantered off along the road. For the next hour a

gang of Thrusk's flunkies rode at a safe distance
behind them, shouting threats and insults.

They were leagues from Firnesse before Wat
Hedgebury could speak at all. Then he just said,
"Thank you, sir," in a small whisper. His hands
were *still* shaking.

The old man did not look around. "You are
most welcome, lad. I enjoyed that little episode
more than I have enjoyed anything for a long
time. And you earned it."

He did not explain that remark then. They
stopped at the first Eastfare estate they came to,
and he had his new friend throughly scrubbed
and clad in fresh clothes. He ordered the old
ones burned, and perhaps his own also. And it
was there, when the two of them were eating a
meal in a humble farmhouse kitchen, that he
first spoke the magic name of Ironhall.

"You have wonderful agility," he said. "You
most certainly have courage. And you have a
sense of justice. I think you would make an excellent Blade to serve your King."

The future Stalwart had laughed heartily, convinced that the knight was joking.

The old man smiled, knowing that he was being misunderstood. "Was Owain a relative?"

"No, sir."

"Have you any family at all?"

Wat shook his head, munching bread and
cold roast goose.

"How old are you?"

"Almost thirteen, master."

" 'Almost' may be good enough. We must put you somewhere out of those men's reach. The Baron is just a windbag, but that Thrusk is pure poison. He carries grudges. Somewhere far away. Do you really want to be a minstrel all your life, singing for the gentry, cap in hand for a copper penny? Sleeping in stables, trudging winter roads in leaky boots? Wouldn't you rather be one of the gentles yourself?"

And Wat—he was always to remember that stunning moment when he realized that this talk was not just a gentleman's joke—stopped chewing and stared in disbelief.

Sir Vincent shuddered. "Close your mouth, boy!"

After a swallow that almost choked him, the boy whispered, "Me?"

"You."

"*A gentleman?* Is that possible?"

"I'd say the King's right hand itself is possible. If you want, I'll take you to Ironhall. Grand Master will accept you, I promise. You're much too good to waste." He chuckled at the boy's stare of disbelief. "Weather looks good. They don't expect me back at Valglorious for a few days yet. We can start right now if you're ready."

Unpleasant Journey

SKULDIGGER'S COACH-AND-FOUR MADE NO great speed along the dusty, rutted trail, but for comfort it could not be surpassed. It could seat four people at ease and six at a pinch on softly padded benches upholstered in mauve silk. Yet Emerald wished fervently that she were back in Wart's smelly wagon. Thrusk's blow had left the side of her head swollen and throbbing; she was going to have a black eye from it.

The bait had been taken. If the mysterious Sir Snake was hoping to catch her kidnappers red-handed, he had better pounce soon. While she hated to concede a point to anyone as odious as Doctor Skuldigger, it did seem that he had won the bout, that Snake had been outwitted and must still be watching the wagon. She had last seen it being driven by one of Skuldigger's coach guards clad in Wart's cap and jerkin, with Murther beside him sporting Emerald's bonnet.

To increase her misery, she was a prisoner in

a vehicle screaming with magic. It came from the coachman on his box, the grooms on the back, the remaining man-at-arms on the roof. At times she could even hear it from Thrusk's escort when they rode close.

Skuldigger sat on the rear bench of the carriage, facing his two captives, and for a long time he seemed to be lost in thought, staring at nothing with the woebegone look of a basset hound. After an hour or so, the carriage left the rutted trail which was flattered with the name of highway and began following a barely visible path over the rolling moorland. Now it moved slowly, often splashing through shallow ponds and streams. The wind brought a scent of the sea. He roused himself.

"Well, Sister Emerald, I am ready to hear your—"

"I told you last night, Doctor! If I were a White Sister I should never have been riding in that wagon."

He groaned. "Aw? Emerald, you must never, never interrupt me when I am speaking, or I shall be forced to punish you. If you do not answer all my questions courteously and truthfully, without attempt to mislead or omit pertinent information, then you will have only yourself to blame for what you will have to endure in consequence. Is this not correct, Sister Swan?"

Swan had been staring fixedly out the window. She turned toward Emerald but did not meet her eye. "He will have you flogged or branded. He is utterly without compassion, utterly ruthless. He is also completely crazy, but no one can defy him. Resist him and he will break you."

Skuldigger showed no resentment at being called a madman. "A very exact description of the situation—if you disobey you must be punished. You cannot hope to escape from Quagmarsh, where we are headed, so you may as well accept reality now and save yourself unnecessary suffering. I cannot use sorcery on you without destroying the abilities I need in you, so I am forced to resort to brutality." His tone and manner implied this was an unavoidable tragedy. "Marshal Thrusk supplies this quite willingly and in much greater quantities than you can possibly withstand. Clear?"

"Yes, Doctor." Her mouth was very dry.

"Sister Swan cooperates with me, you see? Her daughter, Belle, is a beautiful child, but she has the sort of fair skin that scars easily. Her mother knows that I left strict orders to feed the girl to the chimeras tomorrow, so it is essential that I return safely to Quagmarsh in good time to countermand those orders."

Swan was staring out the window again. She seemed to be weeping.

"Now, Emerald," Skuldigger moaned, "I want the true story. I am aware that Sister Swan cannot judge your truthfulness under the present circumstances, but when we reach Quagmarsh, I shall ask you if you lied to me. Swan can tell me then how truthfully you respond; if her reports are not favorable, terrible things will happen to you."

Emerald had made a grave mistake in worming even a small part of the story out of Wart. If she were still as ignorant as she had been when she left Oakendown, she could talk freely. Now she knew things that she must not mention: Sir Snake, attempts on the King's life that were not generally known, poisoned shirts, ensorcelled saddles, and even previous knowledge that Swan and her daughter had been kidnapped. If she lied she would be detected. If she refused to talk, she would be tortured.

"I am not a Sister. I was—for one whole day. Then I was expelled. The Companionship was shipping me home in that farm cart."

The improbability of this tale made Doctor Skuldigger even sadder than before. "But you must have known you were being set out as lure for me?"

"No. I never heard of you—I knew nothing about you. And still don't."

He pouted. "Expelled for what cause?"

"I witnessed a sorcery and was ordered to lie about it. And wouldn't."

"Expelled? Expelled when half the country is screaming for White Sisters to protect them from myself and some of my colleagues? You wouldn't be expelled if you committed multiple murders. Then you just happen to be billeted in the same room as Mistress Murther, who is my agent looking out for potential recruits. Are you so stupid that you believe this to be mere coincidence?"

"Not now I don't. Now I think as you do, that I was deliberately set out as bait. But I am an innocent victim. I never saw the boy before and know nothing about him except what he told me." She had spoken the truth so far.

"The boy will be questioned, do not worry." The Doctor uttered another of his moans. "Aw? I am sure you are right. It is tragic that you must suffer so, but the fault lies entirely with the King and that bullyboy of his called Snake. He is a fool, though, and easily outwitted. Swan could find no trace of magic on you or the wagon or even the boy. I hope you do not disagree with her evaluation?" The bleary, red-rimmed eyes peered inquiringly at Emerald.

"I detected no sorcery." Except an indefinable something about Wart . . . but lots of people bore such imbalances. It was certainly too faint to be of any importance.

Skuldigger showed his lower teeth in what was apparently a smile. "So Snake was relying on purely secular means to track you, my dear, and I have now outsmarted him. It is not the first time, and I am sure it will not be the last."

"I am sure you are right, master." Still she was telling no lies!

"When Murther sent word that she had located a suitable recruit, I suspected right away that you were a decoy. I detected the unsubtle hand of Snake, but I came anyway, because the man is nothing but a trained sword swinger, without finesse or ability. I suppose that eventually even the King will see that. But perhaps not, because Ambrose himself is a bigger fool than any. For years this fair land of Chivial has been molested by the evil Baels, and when someone attempts to do something about them, he is harried and persecuted. The King is not just a fool but also a profligate, power-crazy tyrant!"

Swan glanced very briefly at Emerald and then returned to staring out the window.

Emerald said, "I don't think I understand, Doctor." She would rather have the madman gloating over his own cleverness than interrogating her.

"The Baels, child! For years these pirates and slavers have molested our coasts at will. Foolish Ambrose can do nothing about them. Only superior sorcery will defeat them; yet I and others like me, who strive to develop this magic, are hounded by his government. Such research takes years and vast amounts of gold, yet we are persecuted by rapacious tax gatherers. And when some of my colleagues attempted to remonstrate, they were denounced as traitors!"

He was probably referring to the Night of Dogs, but Emerald did not need to comment. He was ranting, paying no attention to her or Swan.

"Now this despot is attempting to put us out of business altogether and ban our research! Well, we have ways of dealing with such incompetents, and you will have the honor of assisting us. Soon, I promise you, the crown will sit on the head of a three-year-old boy, and a regency council will certainly display more sense than his father ever did. The bungling Snakes and Durendals will be swept aside, and the government of this country will be in the hands of more rational men. Aw? I believe we have arrived."

Reluctant Ally

HOW MANY HOURS HAD HE BEEN LYING IN THE wagon? His feet were as numb as his hands now, but the waves of pain around the gag in his mouth were worse than ever.

The wagon had left the road, and that was bad—very, very bad. That was disaster. He had laid the best trail he could, as he had been instructed, but it had turned out to be the *wrong* trail. At Three Roads he had bribed four separate boys to look out for men wearing cat's-eye swords and tell them about the mysterious Mistress Murther and Doctor Skuldigger, a man with a Grimshank connection. *Do not forget to mention Thrusk!* he had warned them all.

And that had been a terrible mistake. The wagon was rocking over hillocks, it was splashing through streams and ponds. It was not on the public road at all. It was not going to Firnesse, so when Snake and his men learned that they had been hoodwinked, they would go looking in the wrong direction entirely.

That was exactly the sort of foul-up Sir Vincent had predicted.

About halfway on that other journey, the one from Ironhall to Valglorious, and about the time Stalwart realized that Snake was serious when he said they were going to ride right across the country that day, they picked up another of the Old Blades, Sir Chefney. He had been a fencer of renown and Deputy Commander back when Montpurse was leader. There was something utterly unreal in riding stirrup to stirrup with such men and casually saying, "Tell me about the times you won the King's Cup, brother."

Brother!

Chefney laughed. "Just twice—353 and 357. What was different those years was that Durendal wasn't competing. I came second to him a couple of times, but I could never beat him. Never did, not once, even in practice. Then Jarvis came on the scene and turned me into a has-been. I hear you're pretty fast yourself, brother."

Brother!

After twelve hours in the saddle, Wart staggered into the great hall at Valglorious and the arms of Sir Vincent. The old man's beard was pure white now, but his back was still straight and his eyes were bright as a child's. Indeed they glistened and Wart could hardly see them for his own tears. Brushing aside the congratulations, he fell on his knees and took Vincent's hand to kiss.

"It is your doing, sir! If I have achieved anything, it was because I had to be worthy of your trust."

"Get up, you young rascal!" the knight said gruffly. "And no more of this 'sir' talk. You're my brother in the Order now."

"Never!" Wart said. "If you will not allow 'sir,' then I shall call you 'father' and nothing less."

"Listen to that!" Snake said. "I can't wait to hear how he talks when he starts chasing girls. Are you going to feed us, brother, or lay our bones in the ossuary?"

"Food's coming," Vincent said. "I don't know any man who can eat like you and stay so thin. If you were my horse I would worm you. But first I want to see what Ironhall has made of this minstrel trash I picked up. Come along, all of you."

"Good idea," Snake said blithely. "Work out some of the knots."

It was unbelievable. It was inhuman! Twelve hours in the saddle and they expected a man to fence? Of course they did. He was a Blade now.

The great hall, to which Vincent now led his guests, could have been used for horse racing or indoor archery. Lit that evening only by flickering candles, its walls soared up into mysterious darkness. There would be ample space, but light was going to be a problem. Even with blunt épées, fencing practice was never totally without danger. By the time they reached the senior class at Ironhall, future Blades scorned the use of padded garments or even face masks. Swordsmanship was not a game to them, and a few bangs with a steel bar taught the importance of a good defense like nothing else could. But Ironhall had an octogram and skilled enchanters ready to treat injuries right away. Valglorious almost certainly did not, so what Stalwart's new brothers were proposing seemed utterly crazy. He wondered if it was his fencing they wanted to test or his courage. Poking out a friend's eye would be a poor start to his career in the Guard.

Jerkins and doublets were shed. Wart faced off against Sir Vincent. His instinct was to let the old man win, of course, but he knew that such courtesy would be no kindness in this case. Furthermore, to deceive any man about his fencing ranked as mortal sin in the Blades' code, and these men would not be taken in. He began cautiously, parrying every stroke and making little effort to riposte until he could judge the light. The swords clattered and clanged. Then he flashed in with Rainbow, one of his favorite routines. It was easy.

"A hit!"

Vincent laughed. "It was indeed. Try that again."

Clink, clatter—Cockroach! "Another!" *There! This is what you made of me!*

"I'm dead!" the old man agreed. "I think my judgment has been vindicated." He looked to Chefney. "Show us how your wind is standing up to the years, brother?"

"Not worth a glob of pond slime," Chefney retorted. "Snake, you found this whippersnapper. You cut him down to size for us."

"Obviously I must teach him respect for his betters," said Snake, removing his doublet. He accepted the épée, raised it briefly in salute, and then went for Wart like a wildcat.

Back and forth the two of them danced on the flagstones, and their blades rang to the rafters. Now Boy Wonder had a real battle on his hands, because Snake was only two years past his release from the Guard, still very much in his prime. He had never won the King's Cup, but he had always been a respected fencer and he could call on many times Stalwart's experience. Every routine had its counter, and Snake knew them all—Violet . . . Willow . . . Steeple . . . Butterfly. . . . Lunge and parry, engagement and envelopment and *froissement* . . .

How about *Woodpecker*, then?

Snake yelped in surprise as Stalwart's blade tapped the side of his throat. "Do that again!"

Clatter . . . *Vulture?*

"Ouch!"

"Sorry," Stalwart said. "A little harder than I intended."

"Again!" Snake roared, sounding seriously annoyed now.

He was outclassed, though. Four times his new protégé scored, and at last he conceded defeat, puffing mightily.

Wart had beaten Snake himself! Wow! What would they say back in Ironhall if they knew that?

"Give me!" Chefney said, reaching for the blade. "Show *me* how you do it, brother."

To go up against the great Chefney would have seemed like insanity a mere ten minutes ago, but now Stalwart's dander was up. He fizzed with excitement. "At you, then!"

Clitter, clatter . . . Oops . . . "A hit!" Stalwart admitted. "Again!"

Another hit . . .

And another . . . He tried Vulture again, and even Castanet, but nothing worked. After the fifth point he lowered his foil, resisting the temptation to hurl it to the floor. He had forgotten what humiliation felt like. Five to nothing and in about two minutes! The old man was not even breathing hard, and he must be three times Stalwart's age. *Has-been* indeed! Boy Wonder could feel his face burning with shame.

"What's he doing wrong, Chef?" Snake asked. "What did I miss?"

Chefney did not answer him. He spoke instead to Stalwart as the two of them were resuming their doublets. "Where did you get all that complicated rubbish?"

"From Sir Quinn," Stalwart admitted. The recently appointed Master of Rapiers had a collection of highly unusual routines he called Fancy Stuff, which he claimed had won duels against skilled opponents in the past. He warned that they must only be used as a last resort, and he taught them only to the best, those who had already mastered the standard Ironhall style. They had worked against Snake well enough.

Snake was not Chefney.

"Forget the flimflammery!" Chefney said sourly. "Stick with what works. If you can't beat an outsider with Ironhall basics, then nothing is going to save you."

"Yes, brother," Stalwart said as humbly as he could, donning his cloak. "I'll remember." *No more Fancy Stuff!*

"Good. Do that and you'll be a serious contender for the Cup inside three years."

"I *will*?" Stalwart asked, suspecting mockery.

"Certainly. Your speed's incredible—lightning in a bottle—and your footwork's the best I've seen since Durendal. You'd have wiped me clean just now if you hadn't tried to be so fandangle clever." The expert turned away, leaving Stalwart gaping. "Where's that meal you promised, Vincent?"

Snake grinned. "I'm going to start putting money on him now."

"You won't get any takers here," Sir Vincent said proudly, thumping Stalwart's shoulder. "Never met a wolf looked so like a rabbit."

So losing didn't matter after all. It was a gloriously unbelievable ending to an unbelievable day. Unfortunately the deadly Sir Stalwart spoiled it all by falling asleep at the table with his head among the dishes. He did not wake even when Snake and Chefney carried him upstairs and put him to bed.

Sir Vincent was a knight in the Order, castellan of Valglorious, regent of the Duchy of Eastfare, member of the White Star, a baronet in his own right, one of the most honored men in the realm. He was too old to join the Old Blades and fight in the Monster War, even had he not had a dukedom to run. Although he had politely refrained from asking questions when three brother Blades dropped in on him, he knew that theirs was not just a sentimental visit. They wanted something.

The next morning he called them to account. And since this meeting was business and not social, he held it with all four of them standing in the great hall, in front of the gigantic fireplace. There was no one else present. He was dressed more formally than he had been the previous evening; a four-pointed diamond star glinted on his jerkin. Snake, to Wart's great amusement, was flaunting an identical bauble. It had not been in evidence a few minutes earlier, during breakfast.

The thin man outlined the problem of the unknown assassins. Chefney explained how a White Sister was to be offered as bait and how she would be watched during the two or three days she would be made to wait in Tyton. "If no approach is made to her there, then the Companionship will provide transportation to her home, which is near Newhurst. Rather than sending her by stage, though, we thought we would make her seem more vulnerable."

"Let Wart outline this part," Snake said.

So Wart took over the tale, showing that he understood the role he was to play and the various contingency plans Snake and Chefney had devised. He threw in a couple of suggestions of his own, which won thoughtful nods from his superiors.

"And if the evildoers still ignore her," Snake concluded, "we shall have her watched for two or three weeks after she arrives in Newhurst. But that may be too late. The King may well be dead by then."

Vincent's face had been growing darker and darker. Now he said, "And what do you want from me?"

Snake nodded to Wart to answer that one, too.

"Well, sir, mostly we need a reasonable excuse for me to be driving a wagon south from Oakendown by a fairly roundabout route, so the conspirators have time to organize the grab, if that's what they decide to do. We hope you will loan us the horse and wagon and let me pose as one of your hands. Your knowledge of the area, of course . . . a really rusty, hacked-up sword if you can find one, and . . ." He wilted under the old man's glare. "And your blessing on our venture, father."

"You *cut* that *out*!" the old castellan snapped. "I am not your father, and if I were I would forbid this nonsense absolutely." He turned his anger on Snake. "No blessing from me! I think the entire scheme is disgraceful and unworkable. The trick you propose playing on the girl is utterly base, unworthy of our Order. The danger to both her and the boy is unconscionable. He'll end in a ditch with his throat cut. I cannot imagine how you can be so unscrupulous as even to consider such a monstrous fraud."

His visitors exchanged glum glances.

"Because we're desperate," Snake said. "Four attempts in the last month? Leader is going out of his mind. We honestly believe they, whoever *they* are, will succeed next time or the one after."

Vincent bent his head and began to pace back and forth before the great stone mantel. After a moment he stopped and scowled at Snake. "You're telling me the Companionship has agreed to this?"

"With distaste, obviously, but they would rather stage a kidnapping under controlled conditions than lose any more Sisters completely. Mother Superior selected the—hmm—the victim herself and has been cooperating with Brother Chefney in the planning."

What Snake had told Wart the previous day was that Mother Superior's audience with the King had been extremely noisy, with much royal shouting. The Blades on duty outside the door had reported that she came out in tears. But she was cooperating now.

Vincent grunted and went back to his pacing. Then he reached a decision. "No. I will not be associated with such deceit. I bid you good chance, brothers, and safe journey."

He was not the sort to be talked into changing his mind once he had made it up. Snake shrugged hopelessly and looked at Chefney to see if he had any suggestions, but it was Wart who spoke up.

"It shocked me, too, sir, until I thought about it. I haven't met a White Sister yet, but I'm told they're honorable, dedicated women. I agree that it's unkind to involve one without her consent, but her sisters in the Companionship are probably being tortured into cooperating and one of them has a child with her. If this Sister Emerald is at all typical, she should support our efforts wholeheartedly. She won't be in as much danger as I will, because she will be the prize.

And if it is me you are worried about, remember that I am the only man in the Guard who has a hope of pulling this off. It has to be me. Binding leaves a scar and it also marks a man so the Sisters can detect him. Anyone but me will be slaughtered on the spot. Me, I'm just a kid. Who could suspect me of being dangerous? Only yesterday, father, I swore to set my life as nothing to—"

Vincent's face had turned very red. "*I am not your father!*"

Wart shouted right back at him. "Then stop behaving as if you are! Think, *brother!* When you were my age and a senior at Ironhall, if you had been offered this chance to serve your king, wouldn't you have grabbed it with both hands, danger or no danger? This is what Blades are for! You made me what I am. Don't destroy me now!"

"Destroy you? *They* will destroy you!—these two scoundrels. Boy, I'm as old as both of them put together and I say they've dazzled you with all their clever planning—contingency this and supposition that. It's too complicated. They've forgotten that chance is elemental, and sooner or later chance always outsmarts us, all of us. Something totally unforeseen will trip you up and ruin it all."

That should have been the end of it. Wart thought it was the end, and it was with no great hope that he added, "Well, we'll do the best we can without you, sir. If I die, I'll be in good company. Twenty-four brothers in the last half year! That's one a week."

Vincent glared at him, then at Snake. "You're really determined to go through with this whether I help or not?"

"I have no choice, brother."

"Of course we'll do it," Wart said, *"brother."*

"Flames and death!" The old man shook his head. "Then we'd better talk about it a little more. . . . Let me get my steward." He stalked over to a bell rope.

Under his breath, Snake hissed, "You sing a sweet song, minstrel."

"Don't I!" Wart whispered happily.

He had won Sir Vincent over, but the song he sang had turned out to be his own funeral dirge.

Chimeras

THE COACH HALTED ON VERY MARSHY GROUND near the edge of a wood. Descending the steps behind Doctor Skuldigger, Emerald found herself enveloped in dense clouds of insects. Horses lashed tails and angrily splashed their hooves in the mud. Certainly the sea was not far off, for its tangy scent was detectable even under the fetid stench of swamp. The view inland was blocked by a gentle rise in the land, but no buildings or landmarks explained why this place was significant. As soon as Swan came down, one of the grooms folded up the steps and closed the door.

Swan's eyes were red with weeping. She stood hunched and downcast, making no effort to sidle out of the group, even ignoring the tormenting bugs. Emerald hoped the two of them might move off by themselves so she could ask a few private questions. She also wanted to escape the nerve-racking shriek of sorcery emanating from the men.

"Herrick and Thatcher, you will return with me," Skuldigger decreed. Without a word the remaining guard clambered up beside the coachman on the box. Why were all these men so surly? It must have something to do with the magic they bore.

The four horses leaned into their collars and the big vehicle began to squelch forward. In moments it gathered speed and dwindled into the distance.

One of the grooms headed toward the woods on a very faint trail that had been trampled through the reeds and sedge. Swan followed him without being told. Emerald hesitated, wondering if she should make a break for freedom now, whether she could outrun the men and hide in the trees.

Then something roared in the wood—from the sound of it, something very large and very fierce. The groom leading the way screamed and came racing back, with Swan close behind, both of them looking over their shoulders. Whatever it was roared again and the undergrowth swayed. Emerald caught a whiff of sorcery like a foul animal stink.

"There's one in the trees!" the other man yelled. "It's coming!"

"No need for panic!" said Skuldigger testily.

From a pouch at his belt he produced a small golden object, which he put to his lips like a whistle. The result was not sound but a blast of magic, a bolt of pain straight through Emerald's head, making her cry out. *Something* went crashing away through the wood. There was a splash in the distance, silence.

"*What* was that?" she demanded.

All the men ignored her. Swan said, "A chimera," and turned her back, unwilling to explain what a chimera was.

"It's gone now!" Skuldigger sighed. "Bring the prisoners." He stalked off with his sword swinging at his side.

Swan followed him. The grooms, Herrick and Thatcher, closed in on Emerald as if intending to resort to violence without further ado. Slipping and splashing and cursing her ill-fitting shoes, she let herself be shepherded after the Doctor.

The wood itself turned out to be a mere fringe of shrubbery and sickly saplings along the bank of a river or tidal channel—dark, still, and unwholesome. The far bank was similarly wooded. On the black mud beach lay a flat-bottomed boat, which doomed any remaining hope that Snake and his men might be able to track the kidnappers back to their lair. Skuldigger climbed over the side and paused to look with distaste at the seating. It was wet.

Granted that the punt lay in shadow, the day

was too hot for the thwarts to stay damp very long. Recalling the splash she had heard a few moments earlier, Emerald went to inspect the narrow mud flat beside the boat. She did not have to look hard to find the footprint. There was only one, for the crushed weeds nearby would not hold an impression. Here the chimera had come, fleeing from Skuldigger's magical whistle, and here it had planted one foot as it dived into the river. The indentation was very deep, made by a heavy animal moving fast, but it was still clearly visible, for the water seeping in had not yet filled it. It was about the length of a human print, although much wider, and it had the same five toes grouped together at the front. She was no woodsman, but her father had often shown her animal tracks in snow and identified them for her, and this was like nothing she had ever seen. Each of those five clearly defined toes must bear a talon as big as her thumb. A bear? She was not familiar with bear spoor.

She took a few steps back along the way the thing had come, trying to imagine what sort of monster might have inspired such fright in Swan and the two grooms. Hearing a drone of flies like a pipe organ in the trees to one side of the trail, she turned that way.

"Emerald, where are you going?" Skuldigger called.

"To look at . . . *this!*"

This was a carcass, bloody and shredded, with bones and meat scattered around. Scraps of white fat and gray fur lay in a separate pile. The chimera had been interrupted while feeding on whatever that litter of flesh had been.

"Harbor seal," Skuldigger announced, joining her. He sounded almost pleased, less mournful than usual. "I wonder if it wandered into the river or if my pets are venturing out to sea now?"

"Chimeras?"

"I call them that, yes." He was wearing the golden whistle on a gold chain around his neck.

"I do not see," Emerald said as calmly as she could manage, "any signs that the carcass was dragged there." It had been carried in, then. There had been only one splash, one chimera. "How much would a harbor seal weigh, Doctor?"

"This appears to have been an adult male. Substantially more than Marshal Thrusk."

"Chimeras are large animals?"

He uttered a peculiar choking noise that was probably a laugh. "Large, yes. Animals . . . not entirely."

The Doctor sat on one of the punt's two thwarts. The women took the other, at his back, while Herrick and Thatcher stripped off their road-stained and uncomfortable livery. Wearing only knee breeches, they waded into the mud and then pushed, heaved, and grunted in efforts to launch the ungainly craft.

"We are a little early for the tide," Skuldigger announced without turning around. "It may be necessary for you two to disembark and—Ah, here we go!"

The boat moved, and once it had started the two men easily slid it the rest of the way into the water. They scrambled aboard, mud caked from the knees down, and grabbed up poles in time to stop the awkward craft from running aground on the far bank. Then they turned her and began poling her along the channel. Although there was no visible current, Emerald decided that they were heading downstream. She was judging by the height of the sun at her back, a feeling that the day was aging into late afternoon, and knowledge that the sea lay to the east. After a few moments the channel curved around so that she had the sun in her face. Another channel came in on the right. At that point she gave up trying to memorize the way through the maze. Thatcher and Herrick heaved on their poles, working their hearts out. She at least could fan the flies away from her face. Their sweating torsos were peppered with bugs like black freckles.

Skuldigger glanced around briefly. "I advise you to sit nearer the center," he moaned.

Emerald realized that he and the two boatmen were keeping careful watch on the black, oily water and the sinister woods. She hastily moved away from the side. Swan had needed no warning. The punt suddenly seemed very narrow. "Can a chimera snatch people out of boats?"

Swan just nodded.

Emerald tried again. "Doctor, what exactly is a chimera?"

Without turning his head, he replied in a loud lament, as if he were addressing a large funeral. "Quagmarsh used to be a fishing village. I cannot call it a 'humble' fishing village, because in fact it was extremely arrogant, denying allegiance to any lord and claiming an ancient history. There was a token stockade around it, but the foolish inhabitants relied for their safety on the assumption that only they had the specialized geographic knowledge and boats of sufficiently shallow draft to navigate these marshes. Possibly they also assumed that they owned nothing worth stealing. Aw! They learned the magnitude of their folly about ten years ago, when a party of Baelish raiders came in on a spring tide. Baels are slavers and their longships draw very little water. They stripped Quagmarsh of everyone except old people. You can still see where they tried to burn it down, but there must have been rain that day. The survivors fled inland and Quagmarsh stood empty until my colleagues and I moved in a few months ago."

He paused to stare suspiciously at an unexplained ripple until the punt was safely past it. "If the Baels would just try to repeat their success now, the results would be very interesting, a foretaste of what will happen when I launch my attack on Baelmark itself. The most important thing you must learn in Quagmarsh, Emerald—other than total loyalty to myself and instant obedience to my wishes—is to stay inside the stockade at all times. This is true even in daylight, but at night it is essential. Several people have ignored that rule and paid dearly for their imprudence, including two of your predecessors. We rarely find more than fragments of bloodstained fabric or some well-gnawed bones."

After a moment he added, "The same fate befalls any outsider who wanders close to the village. This may seem unkind, but it is the fault of King Ambrose. While he persecutes us, we are forced to defend ourselves as best we can with our limited resources. Chimeras are always hungry. This must have something to do with their extraordinary growth, which I cannot as yet explain."

This time the silence remained unbroken. The punt moved on. Apparently the lecture was over, but he had not said exactly what a chimera was or looked like. Swan would know, but she was clearly too cowed to speak at all.

Quagmarsh

THE FIRST SIGN OF THE VILLAGE WAS A LOW DOCK of rotting wooden pilings lining the left-hand shore. Behind that stood a wooden palisade, so mossy and ramshackle that it seemed like part of the forest. When Herrick and Thatcher brought the punt in against the wharf and held it there with their poles, Skuldigger removed the golden whistle from his neck and dropped the chain over the head of the taller of the two, whichever one he was. "Go back and wait for the Marshal. Obey his orders. If he does not come, do not wait long enough to miss the tide."

"Master." The man's reply was little more than a grunt.

With the tide in, it was possible to step from the side of the punt straight onto the dock, and thus Emerald followed Swan and the Doctor ashore. The bank was treacherous, a mixture of mud and decayed timber, and in some places the pilings had collapsed to let the soil slide away, leaving gaps like giant bite marks. Nevertheless Swan took off at a run for the gate, going in search of her daughter. Skuldigger strode along behind her, making no effort to call her back.

Emerald followed more cautiously. She was unimpressed by the palisade leaning over her, which had obviously been built many years ago out of the spindly trunks of local trees. It was a mossy, half-rotten fence, not much more than head height, sagging like the flesh on a dowager's neck. She could not imagine how such a wreck could keep out monsters capable of killing and eating full-grown seals. Anyone could knock a hole through that if she had to.

Just before the Doctor reached the gate, two middle-aged men and a young woman came hurrying out. They greeted him warmly—very warmly in the woman's case. Flames! It had never occurred to Emerald that there could be a Mistress Skuldigger. Would she be as crazy as her husband? This question should soon be answered, because the men vanished inside, chatting busily, while the lady waited for Emerald.

First impressions were not favorable. Her rose-and-gold gown was crafted of the finest silk and decorated with innumerable sequins and seed pearls—far better suited for court than a backwater in the swamps. As a concession to reality, the toes of black leather boots showed under the hem of its widely spread skirt, but nothing of the lady herself was visible, being hidden by long sleeves, white gloves, and a red straw hat inside a veil of muslin that completely enveloped her head like a bag. Granted that the overall effect was bizarre, the outfit was practical enough to protect her from both insects and the mire underfoot. She did catch the eye in a little place like this.

"I am Sister Carmine!" she announced in the imperious tones of a herald proclaiming the entry of the Gevilian ambassador. Her face remained a blur behind the muslin.

"Sister Emerald, Sister." Emerald had realized at some point in this interminable day that if her expulsion from Oakendown had been a fraud, as Wart admitted, then she was entitled to ignore it and claim the rank she had earned.

"Welcome to Quagmarsh, Sister."

"My visit here is not by choice."

"Come, I will show you around." Sister Carmine turned and led the way to the gate, being careful not to let her skirt brush against any of the debris. "Choice or not, here you will be privileged to assist in a magnificent extension of the frontiers of human knowledge, combined with a struggle for personal freedom against tyrannical oppression." That answered the question. She was at least as crazy as her husband—birds of a feather flip together.

Inside the gateway, hidden from outside view, lay another punt and two small boats.

There was no street as such, merely narrow passages between squalid huts of wattle and thatch. The air stank of sewage.

Waving away the swarming insects, Emerald said, "Pray explain to me the magic in the amulets Marshal Thrusk and his men wear. I am much relieved to be free of it at last."

"Amulets?" Mistress Skuldigger laughed gaily. "They wear no amulets, child! They have themselves been bespelled with loyalty to Doctor Skuldigger. It is one of his greatest magics, based on the enthrallment sorcery that the Baels use to tame their slaves. The Baels are satisfied to turn their victims into human sheep, incapable of doing anything except obey orders. Doctor Skuldigger has succeeded in imposing absolute obedience without damaging the subjects' intelligence—not to any great extent that is. Yet the tyrant Ambrose seeks to crush all such progress! His oppression is intolerable. It has taken Doctor Skuldigger many years and hundreds of attempts to perfect this sorcery, and the value of it to society could be inestimable."

Well now, there was a debatable statement! The value of such a spell to the sorcerers who owned it would certainly be beyond measure, but Emerald shuddered at the thought of the evil being made available to anyone who could afford it. Landowners would enslave their workers, householders their servants; generals would make troops fearless. . . . This was exactly the sort of magical barbarity the King was trying to stamp out.

"I cannot imagine why a man like Marshal Thrusk would submit to such treatment."

Inside her veils, Mistress Skuldigger laughed. "He did not know he was submitting. A year or so ago he came to the Priory to have a wound healed, a nasty puncture made by a pitchfork tine. Of course Doctor Skuldigger recognized his value right away and enlisted him."

"Thrusk did not mind being tricked like that?"

"He cannot complain. He recruited all his men as well—the Baron's men, really. And the Baron, too, is now a supporter."

Her name, her choice of colors, her burning enthusiasm—they all proved beyond doubt that fire was Carmine's dominant manifest element. Wart had said that there must be at least one Sister cooperating willingly with the traitors. A little thought showed the logic of that, because the captors would need to know when the captives were lying to them. Carmine was that traitor, the Sister who had married the corrupt sorcerer. Emerald wondered if her dominant virtual element was love, which could make its children do anything. No, in that case she should not be so indifferent to the suffering her husband's work created. Chance, more likely. Fire-chance people were so unpredictable and uncontrollable that the Companionship rarely admitted them.

Carmine followed a complex winding path through the shacks. Some of them were collapsed ruins; others had recently been repaired, and sounds of hammering and sawing not far off suggested that the work continued. The few people in sight were obviously servants and laborers, the telltale discordant whistle of enchantment indicating that they had all been bespelled. But there had to be other inhabitants in this den of horrors. The men who had greeted Skuldigger at the gate must have been colleagues, for eight people were needed to conjure the eight elements. The slaves' loyalty spells would disrupt the balance of elements too much for them ever to work magic. Masters and slaves alike seemed to be prisoners of the monsters roaming the swamps.

"What does a chimera look like?"

"Depends on the ingredients Doctor Skuldigger used to make it. He has warned you about them, I hope?"

"In a general sense. They attack on sight?"

"Oh yes. Most of them are flesh eaters and they all seem to be permanently ravenous. To venture far from the stockade by day is very dangerous. By night it is suicide. You will be eaten alive, and not just by mosquitoes!" Sister Carmine found her own humor irresistibly funny. Love was certainly not a major element in her makeup.

"Why do creatures so powerful not break into the village?"

"Because they were ordered not to do so when they were assembled, of course. Doctor Skuldigger has also made a device that drives them away. Without that we should all be trapped in here forever."

"Only one 'device'? Isn't that rather risky?" If a prisoner could steal that magical whistle. . . .

"We have several copies. You will note," Sister Carmine said, changing the subject abruptly, "that I am not taking you by the shortest route. If you are as sensitive as I am, you will have detected the conjuration presently underway in the elementary. I wish to avoid it."

Emerald had certainly noted it—magic like a stench of rotting fish—and now she could hear chanting. A few moments later her guide led her into a small open area, an irregular patch of weeds and mud that seemed to serve as a village square. A woman was turning a windlass on a well, making horrible squeaking noises, and a gang of four men was repairing thatch on one of the huts.

"Do come and see this!" Carmine said excitedly. "One of our trappers brought in an *otter* this morning! Very rare! Usually they just catch water rats or squirrels. In fact, the trap lines are often quite empty now. The chimeras have scared everything away."

Or eaten everything, Emerald thought. What would happen when there was nothing left for them to eat in the woods?

Carmine stopped at a small open-fronted shed containing a collection of metal cages. She peered into them until she found the one she wanted and then banged on it. The lump of fur in one corner did not move. "There it is. Poor thing! They say its paw is injured and of course they never eat in captivity. I expect Doctor Skuldigger will want to use it tonight, before it starves itself to death."

Emerald did not ask *Use how?* She did not want to know. She was more interested in two solid posts outside and the rusty chains dangling from them.

"And this?"

Although Sister Carmine's face was concealed by her veil, her smile could be heard in her voice. "Well, those serve several purposes. New recruits usually have to be restrained until Doctor Skuldigger and his assistants have time to attend to them. On occasion they also serve as a whipping post. You have met Marshal Thrusk?"

Emerald did not answer.

"This way." Sister Carmine set off through the weeds in her fine gown. "You will find that the cost of defiance rises swiftly. Doctor Skuldigger will question you later, and I expect he will introduce you to your duties. They are very simple and quite harmless if performed correctly."

Past two or three more huts, they came to a woman sitting on a bench outside a doorway, cuddling a child of about two. It was Sister Swan, and both she and her daughter were so intent on each other that they did not notice the arrivals until Carmine spoke.

"There you are!" she said cheerfully.

Swan jumped. The child screamed. And screamed. She tried to burrow into her mother's neck, screaming all the time. Swan picked her up and ran into the hut, just as another woman came out to see what was happening. It was quite understandable that a two-year-old girl might be frightened by a woman with a bag over her head, but somehow Emerald thought that Belle knew exactly who was under the veil, and that was why she had screamed. And was still screaming inside the hut, despite all her mother could do to calm her.

But the other woman—large, plump, grandmotherly . . .

"Cloud!"

"Emerald!"

They fell into each other's arms.

"Oh, how nice!" Carmine declaimed. "I am so glad you know each other. This will help you to settle down in your new home, Emerald."

Stalwart Unbound

THE WAGON BROKE ITS REAR AXLE ON A ROCK and tipped. The barrels slid, broke open the tailgate, and fell out, one after the other, exploding in a fog of powdered garlic. Fortunately Stalwart was on the uphill side, or he would certainly have been flattened. As he began to move, he expected the noose around his neck to choke him, but the rope had been tied around one of the barrels, so it went with him. Trussed so he could do nothing to save himself, he slid within a torrent of bags and clothes and one archlute to land in the heap of staves and garlic.

"Now you've done it!" Murther screamed. "Thrusk'll have the skin off your back for this. And look at the poor boy! Dead he is!" She came closer, fussing and coughing.

Stalwart was coughing also, and his eyes were full of burning garlic.

"You come here and help, Cordwainer, right now!" she yelled.

The man's voice, farther away, bellowed that he was busy with the horse. Saxon agreed loudly. The woman, to her credit, waded into the debris and dragged Stalwart out. He lay on his side, which was a wonderful experience after so long facedown, and he coughed around the gag. At least his torment in the wagon was over. Almost anything would be better than that. But oh, his eyes!

"Poor boy!" she muttered. She struggled, trying to unfasten the gag, having trouble with Thrusk's knots. "Not our fault. Have to do what we're told, see. 'Don't stop,' he said. 'Take him all the way to the landing if you can.' Well, that's Thrusk for you—mean as they come."

The wagon creaked and settled as Saxon was freed from the shafts.

"Never said we could untie him," the man growled, coming to see.

"Well, and how are we to get him to the landing if we don't? You going to carry him, Cordwainer?"

"Could put him over the horse."

"I'll ride the horse, thank you. Don't you just stand there like a dumb mule. Bring the canteen, if there's anything left in it. Look at his face! And then cut his hands free so—*Look* at his hands, won't you! And his feet'll be no better, I'm sure. Oh, his poor face!"

The woman, querulous sourpuss though she was, treated Stalwart with consideration, wiping his tongue and cracked lips with a wet rag. Had she just put the bottle to his mouth, he would probably have choked himself. He wanted her to wash out his eyes, but he couldn't speak, so he waited.

"Thrusk never say we're to cut him loose, Murther." The man continued his growl, but he was sawing at Stalwart's bonds as he did so.

Stalwart managed a swallow. He must be alive. No one dead could hurt so much.

His troubles were far from over. When his mouth had been cared for and he had drunk his fill, when his eyes had been washed out and he could see again—although still not very well—then it was time for the blood to start returning to his hands and feet. His fingers looked like pig guts, except they were blue. Hurt? His jaw hurt, but the pain of the blood returning to his hands was going to be worse than that. Murther and Cordwainer fretted and muttered and wanted to continue their journey.

"Any more water?" he croaked. The woman handed him the canteen and he emptied it. "Is my lute all right?" What good was a lute to him with his hands like this?

"Looks fine," the man said. He twanged the strings. "That's a wondrous strange-looking lute." Then he stiffened and looked around.

Hooves! Horsemen were coming from the west, from the way the wagon had come—could it be *Snake*? Stalwart struggled upright and managed to stand up with some help from Murther. No, it was not rescue coming. It was Thrusk and his band, who had stayed behind to look out for pursuit. How they must have laughed if they had watched Snake and the Old Blades galloping past along the highway, chasing nothing! Stalwart squared his shoulders and tried to look more defiant than he felt. Should be easy—a dead jellyfish would look more defiant than he felt. His hands were useless balls of sheer agony and his feet not much better. He still wore a rope around his neck, which did not help his dignity much.

Thrusk reined in, enormous on horseback, a mountain against the sky. "Have a nice nap, did you?" he inquired.

"You are a bucket of dog vomit and your mother ate rats."

The big man studied him for a moment and then smiled. He swung a leg over and slid down from his horse. He walked closer, very close. Even on level ground he could fill the sky.

"What did you say, runt?"

"You are a stinking barrel of dog vomit and your mother ate rats raw."

Someone sniggered. Thrusk looked around quickly and the laughter stopped at once.

He turned back to Stalwart. "I'm not allowed to pull that rope over a branch, which is what

I'd like to do, slipgibbet. But I got no orders not to teach you manners."

"You couldn't teach manners to a pig."

"That's quite a lute you got this time. Who'd you steal that one from?"

"It belongs to a friend of mine and you keep your paws off it, you oversized latrine worm!"

The men-at-arms sitting around on their horses were watching to see if their leader would control his temper or hit a man half his size. Stalwart was too mad to care which happened. But he jumped when Thrusk's huge hands grabbed at his neck and in one swift motion ripped his shirt and doublet open to the waist.

"What's that for?"

The giant shrugged. "Just a precaution." He had guessed about Ironhall. Thanks to Snake's cleverness, he had found the only Blade who did not have a binding scar over his heart, but he was still suspicious. "I could flog you, for starters."

"Sure you could, but the reckoning is coming and it's a lot closer than you think. You're in over your head, animal."

Thrusk guffawed and appealed to his audience. "Listen to who's calling me an animal!" Some of them laughed, too, although the humor escaped Stalwart. "Well, you won't be around to sing any songs about it, sonny. The good Doctor has a very special treat in store for you."

Chuckling, Thrusk took the rope and walked back to his horse. Stalwart had no choice but to stagger along behind him on feet that felt like two red-hot bricks.

"Because," Thrusk said as he tied the other end to his saddle, "in future you are going to help guard our little nest for us. You'll be one of our watchdogs. Right now I'm going to take the dog for a run."

Sister Cloud

SISTER CLOUD HAD BEEN EMERALD'S FIRST GUIDE in Oakendown. She was caring and affectionate and did not have a mean bone in her body— and not many other bones either. She was exactly what one would expect an air-love person to be, but she was also exactly what Emerald needed under the present circumstances. She provided sympathy, wash water, fresh clothes, and even her own spare pair of shoes, which were a better fit than those Emerald had been enduring for days. After that she busied herself preparing a meal; she answered questions.

She had been the first Sister kidnapped, back in the spring. Two others taken after her had tried to escape and been eaten by the chimeras. Swan and her daughter had arrived only a few weeks ago. Emerald told them of her own experiences without mentioning Snake's conspiracy.

Cloud, in turn, told her all about Quagmarsh.

There were a dozen sorcerers living there. The Doctor was their leader, or possibly his wife was, because it was her fire element that drove their partnership. He was a water-time person, infinitely patient. The rest of the inhabitants, men and women both, were bespelled to complete obedience.

Emerald asked about chimeras.

"Abominations! Monsters! He makes them by blending people and animals. Wants to mix human intelligence with animal speed and toughness; thinks he can produce an army of unbeatable warriors and send it to conquer Baelmark and win the war."

"What sort of animals?"

"Anything. He keeps experimenting—rats, dogs, birds. Even cattle and pigs."

"So some of them are big?" Emerald, asked, thinking of the seal.

Cloud rolled her eyes. "They're all big and keep getting bigger! They roam the fens, eating everything they can get their claws on. And we're reduced to eating gruel," she added, handing Emerald a bowl. "All we got. Used to get nice fish."

The shadows were growing long, but the bugs were not as bad as before, for the sailors' wind had risen—the breeze sent by the sea at evening to hasten the boats home. It was taken for granted that Emerald would move in with her fellow hostages, although she had the option of cleaning out one of the empty hovels for herself. The hut would suffice for all of them at a pinch, and company was comfort.

As the three women and one child sat around on the floor eating their meager supper, Swan began to join in the talk and show a little vivacity, recovering from the agony of being separated from Belle. She might be a very charming woman in normal times, but her disposition was water-love, which was about the worst possible combination to withstand such an ordeal. Her daughter was unwilling even to look at Emerald or sit anywhere but on her mother's lap. Whatever abuse had provoked their terrors could not be discussed while the child was present.

Obviously neither Cloud nor Swan would offer much resistance to the traitors' demands. Emerald vowed that she, as an earth type, would be made of sterner stuff. She did not think this den of horrors could remain secret very much longer. If Sir Snake and his Old Blades did not find it by themselves, the starving chimeras would lead them to it, preying farther and farther afield until they began eating farmers' livestock. All she had to do was endure until rescue arrived.

"What exactly will I be required to do?" she demanded.

Swan's arms closed protectively around Belle.

Cloud sighed. "Two or three times a day you get called up to what they call the hall—it's just a big hut, really. They will have four or five sacks laid out. Without opening them, you have to say which contain something bespelled and which don't. That's all."

"But you mustn't lie!" Swan cried. "Carmine will ask you if you have lied, and Cloud and I will be given the same test. You can't cheat them."

"Sometimes they give you the same ones again," Cloud agreed. "There's no way to cheat. They get brutal if they think you're trying to deceive them or if you refuse to cooperate." She glanced at Belle, who was sucking a finger. "And you may not be the one they make suffer."

Emerald pointed in horror at the child, and Cloud nodded. *Fair skin that scars easily*, Skuldigger had said.

"I have never heard anything so despicable," Emerald said. "But I have never witnessed a public execution either. I do hope I can start soon."

"Not just watch," Swan snarled. "I'd like to *do* it."

"Slowly," said Cloud, and that was the first time Emerald had ever heard her utter a harsh word against anyone.

Reunion

EMERALD WAS SUMMONED JUST AFTER SUNSET. The messenger was a vacant-faced youth who bore the discordant whistle of the obedience spell. He seemed little better than half-witted, but when they reached their destination he pointed it out to her and ran off into the twilight. Perhaps he was not as stupid as he seemed.

"Hall" was an absurd name for what was merely a large shed. It had no door on its hinges or shutters on its windows; its floor was packed dirt, and birds nested in the rafters of a badly sagging roof. There was no furniture, nowhere to sit. It did boast a stone chimney with a fire crackling on the hearth—ominously, on this still-warm summer night. The long metal rod that lay with one end in the coals looked suspiciously like a branding iron. Emerald stopped just inside the door and surveyed the people standing there.

To her left were Doctor Skuldigger, his over-dressed wife, and two elderly men she did not know. Since they bore no enthrallment spell, she assumed they were sorcerers. Opposite stood Marshal Thrusk and a man-at-arms she recognized from the morning. Between them was Wart, looking much the worse for wear. His eyes were scarlet and swollen, his jaw was puffed out and already turning purple, and his doublet and shirt hung in rags, tattered and grass-stained as if he had been dragged. In an insanity of insanities, he was still clutching his precious archlute, hugging it to him with both arms, not using his hands. But he was still alive, which was a relief; and he smiled lopsidedly at her. She tried to return the smile, being reminded that her face, also, had been bruised by Thrusk's fist, although not nearly so badly as his.

She knew why the conspirators wanted her. She was horribly afraid she also knew why they wanted Wart, because the cage with the otter stood just outside the door. She braced herself for whatever was coming, wishing her lower lip did not keep trying to tremble.

"Aw?" sighed the Doctor. "Here she is. Emerald, I must ask you some questions. Mistress Skuldigger will know if you try to lie to us, and in that case I shall have no choice but to order Marshal Thrusk and man-at-arms Foster to punish you severely. I hope you understand that it is kinder to settle the matter once and for all, and teach you obedience right at the beginning. Now, why were you expelled from Oaken-down?"

She told the truth as she knew it—if she had been the victim of a plot, it had not been know-ingly.

"What do you know of Sir Snake?"

"That he is very stupid and incompetent."

"Ah, that is a lie!" Carmine said.

"Your husband told me so himself."

The only person who found that exchange funny was Wart, who laughed. "Don't believe that one if he tells you day follows—"

Thrusk hit him. It was not a killer blow, just a backhand slap across the mouth, but it must have hurt like fury on top of the existing bruise. Wart staggered and almost dropped his arch-lute. When he straightened, he was blinking away tears of pain; blood trickled from his torn lips.

"Can't you control that animal, Doctor?" Em-erald shouted.

Thrusk laughed. "I'm not as much animal as he's going to be very shortly."

Skuldigger ignored him. "Aw? What do you know about Snake that I did not tell you?"

"Nothing but hearsay," Emerald said. "I never met him."

And so on. For a long time she managed to answer without lying. But finally Skuldigger brought her to a fence she could not jump. "Do you think the boy knew that you were bait?"

"What value have my guesses to you?"

"Aw? You are evading the question. Marshal, you may start using the iron now."

"Yes, sir," The big man stalked over to the hearth. He showed no signs of reluctance or distaste at what he was about to do. "Hold her, Foster."

Before Emerald could turn on her heel and run, the man-at-arms stepped between her and the door, although he did not lay hands on her— not yet. There was nowhere to run to, anyway. She would soon be caught and dragged back, and then either she would be made to suffer more or—much worse!—little Belle would.

"Of course I knew," Wart said hoarsely. "I helped Snake plan it all."

All eyes went to him. He seemed astonishingly unworried by his peril, brave beyond his years, even if he was as old as he claimed. Again Emerald sensed that odd disturbing something about him that had bothered her before, only this time stronger than ever. There was death in it, and a trace of love, time . . . it reminded her of some sorcery she had met somewhere recently.

"Do tell us," Skuldigger moaned, "everything."

Wart shrugged. "What is there to tell? The original idea was Snake's. The King approved it.

Sir Chefney did most of the organizing. I added a couple of details." He showed no signs of lying, but he was certainly bragging. How could he be so bold? Did he have no idea what the otter was for? "We arranged for Emerald to be expelled from the school with no money and no way out except whatever the Sisters offered. Meanwhile, the Sisters were noting who in Tyton was wearing magic, and Mistress Murther's was a very unusual magic. So Emerald was put in her path. Bedroom, I mean. When nothing significant happened, I came forward with the wagon and we trailed the bait. . . . Sorry, Emerald. But it's true, isn't it? We trailed the bait until you swallowed it, Skuldigger. Snake and his men made no effort to stop you, of course, because they wanted you to lead them to your lair—which you did. Thank you. They'll be here shortly." He stopped, grinning as well as his bruise would let him.

He was *not* lying! And now Emerald remembered where she had met that sorcery—on the two Blades she had seen so briefly in the gatehouse. Not that Wart was bound as they had been, but whatever she was detecting on him was strangely similar.

"Mostly true," Sister Carmine said uncertainly. "That last . . . he's not sure . . . but he's not really lying. . . ."

"Explain," wailed the Doctor. "Marshal Thrusk and his men waited behind to see if anyone followed the wagon when it left the main road. No one did. There was no magic on it or on you. If you are not lying to us, then Snake lied to you. You were misled!"

"Well, if you won't believe me," Wart said haughtily, "then I won't play your silly games. So there!"

"Aw? You force us to use force. The iron, Marshal—on the girl."

Thrusk chuckled and bent to test the cool end of the iron with a cautious finger, preparatory to picking it up. Wart turned his archlute so the soundbox was on top. Gripping it by its neck, he raised it like a giant club.

Foster cried out a warning. Thrusk straightened and spun around. They both reached for their swords as Wart swung the long instrument in a great arc overhead. The soundbox crashed into a rafter, exploding in a shower of splinters and inlay—mingled with a deluge of dust and bird droppings. The strings twanged a sonorous dying dirge.

Thrusk guffawed and let go his hilt. "Didn't judge that too well, did you, shrimp?"

Wart reached into the remains of the lute and pulled out a sword. "In the King's name," he shouted—voice quavering with excitement—"I, Stalwart, companion in the Loyal and Ancient Order of the King's Blades, by virtue of the authority vested in me as a commissioner of His Majesty's Court of Conjury, command that all present do now lay down arms and submit to the Royal Justice."

Thrusk drew.

"Kill him!" one of the older men shouted.

Wart said, "If you insist," and bounded across the room.

Fight

IT TOOK STALWART THREE STEPS TO REACH HIS foe—and those three steps seemed to last the rest of eternity, as if all time elementals had fled away in terror and the world would never change again.

On the first step he realized that he was heading into his first-ever real fight with real edges and real points, so he might get killed or maimed very soon. Speed counted for far more than strength, and even Sir Chefney had agreed he was fast, so he would not normally be worried by Thrusk's size. But this was not *normally* at all. His hands were not back to their full strength, and he could not even trust his feet, which were just as important. His neck had not recovered from Thrusk's little dragging games on the horse. He would be slower and weaker than usual; Foster was drawing at his back; both men were wearing armor. *This was going to be very tricky indeed!* As he completed the step he

remembered the latrines at Firnesse and promised himself that he would kill Thrusk if he had
to run up the brute's sword to do it.

On the second step he was assessing the grip
and weight of the weapon he bore. He had
never seen it or touched it before and yet it was
comfortingly familiar, thanks to Snake's fore-
sight.

On that wonderful first morning, just after
they had changed mounts at the first posting inn
and Snake finished outlining the plan, he had
said, "You didn't look at that sword I gave
you."

In Ironhall, drawing a real sword—as op-
posed to a practice weapon—while on horseback was cause for some of the most ghastly
punishments that could be inflicted on a senior,
such as teaching courtly dancing to the soprano
class. But Stalwart wasn't a candidate anymore
and an order was an order, so he drew. The
blade was long and slender, a thrusting sword
almost like a rapier with a single edge added.
He didn't like it much; it was heavier and less
wieldy than a pure rapier and not sturdy
enough for really serious slashing.

Beside, the edge was dull and the point
rounded!

He howled in outrage.

Snake laughed. "No insult intended! That's as
close a match as we could find to the sword
you'll be using on this outing. Want you to get

used to it and shaped up on it, too. You have very little time. We'll give you all the fencing we can—me and Chefney and another couple of hotshots to give you some real workouts. If you're going to need a sword, brother, you're going to need it *fast*. No time for tryouts or practice."

That made sense. Mollified, he waved the weapon a few times and managed to slide it back in the scabbard at full canter. "I prefer a rapier."

"I know. Just thought something a little more versatile might be useful on this outing. This isn't going to be any courtly duel, brother. This'll be mixing it up, roughhousing." Snake reined in to a trot to give the horses a break. "And you can't have the real one. It's inside a lute."

"It's *where*?"

"Inside a lute—an archlute, actually, because we needed the length and the extra weight won't show as much. Lovely thing, cost more than you'll earn in a ten-year stint with the Guard. We had our man disassemble it and hollow out the neck to take the blade. The hilt's inside the soundbox. Then he put it all back together and the varnish is still drying. When in need, smash and draw. Just hope it doesn't bind . . ."

It hadn't, and on his third step Stalwart was assessing his opponent. Thrusk was encased in a helmet and a simple cuirass of breastplate and backplate. There might be gaps where those met, but only a desperate man would gamble on finding them. Below the waist he wore no steel, only breeches well padded with linen, which might not stop a sword stroke completely but would probably save him from serious hurt. Heavy leather riding boots covered his legs to above the knee. There were very few places where Thrusk could be effectively damaged.

He knew how to handle a sword, too, advancing right foot and right shoulder to meet the attack, holding a hand-and-a-half broadsword one-handed, and raising it to a guard position that in Ironhall's own distinctive terminology would be approximately Butterfly. He had it a little too high for his opponent's height, though.

Hoping to make him raise it even farther, Stalwart lunged at Steeple and was parried to Stickleback. Hmm! Man Mountain was quick in spite of his bulk, and his power was hair-raising. There was no resisting his pressure when the blades engaged. Stalwart parried Thrusk's riposte with the neck of the archlute and tried Osprey, which was a tricky compound riposte involving a double feint and a lunge under the opponent's guard. Surprisingly, it did not end with his sword in Thrusk's armpit as it should have done, but he felt his point catch Thrusk's upper arm. Whether it just cut the cloth or nicked the skin he could not tell—and it barely mattered, because Thrusk's recovery put his left foot in the fire. No matter how much a man might trust his boots, that situation would make him lose his focus.

Stalwart left him and spun around with a wild slash that wasn't in the Ironhall repertoire at all—except that instinct was always permitted and in this case the windmill stroke parried a lunge from Foster, who hadn't expected it and obviously didn't know one end of a sword from another. Before he could even go to guard, Stalwart feinted at his eyes with the remains of the archlute and slipped the sword in underneath it to cut his throat.

He turned again with a backward spring away from Thrusk's downward cut, staggering as his feet refused his orders. No one else in the room had even moved a step yet, but this affair had better be settled quickly. He threw the archlute ruin like a javelin. Thrusk let it bounce harmlessly off his armor and lunged, sending Stalwart back yet again. There was very little room here, and if he let himself be cornered he would be a fond memory. He feinted, was parried, and lunged again, very nearly losing an ear. He was fencing like a cripple! Thrusk showed his teeth in a grin. Parry, riposte, parry . . . Lily, Violet . . . *clang—clang—clang—* The man's strength and reach were incredible. Eggbeater. One misjudgment and this flimsy thrusting sword would be cut in half. *Clang—clang—*

He would have to gamble the farm on one roll of the dice.

In desperation he discarded Chefney's advice and reached for Sir Quinn's Fancy Stuff. There was one compound attack called Beartrap that would work best—if it worked at all—for a short man against a very tall opponent. Stalwart lunged, parried, feinted, and ducked under Thrusk's riposte to cut at his right leg, slicing through his boot just above the knee as if he were carving meat. *(Thank you, Snake, for giving me a sword with an edge!)* The hamstring parted; Thrusk cried out and toppled. Even better—as he sprawled forward and Stalwart straightened, for an instant Thrusk had his head back to expose a glimpse of naked throat under his beard. Stalwart rammed his sword in past the collarbone, down among lungs and gullet and major blood vessels. The weapon was almost wrenched out of his hand as Thrust completed his fall, face-first into the floor, but that just meant that the blade was able to do more damage in there.

It was done! It was over! He was bubbling so hard with excitement that he could barely keep from dancing. That was what a real fight was like? And the battle was a long way from over yet. Sir Hawkney had told him that after the

Night of Dogs he hadn't been able to sit down for two days.

He kicked Thrusk's helmet. "Die, you dreg!" he shouted. "You hear me, brute? You're dying. I killed you. I wish I could do it again."

Flight

SORRY ONLY THAT HE COULD NOT GLOAT longer over the death throes, he turned to survey the glazed eyes and open mouths of the five spectators. Obviously they had never seen a Blade in action before. One boy and two dead or dying men, and it had taken less than a minute. Skuldigger still wore his sword.

"I told you to throw down your weapons!" Unfortunately Stalwart's voice came out as a shrill squeak.

That didn't matter. Screaming in terror, the four traitors turned and rushed for the doorway with the woman in the lead. Emerald, bless her, stuck out a foot and tripped her. Skuldigger fell on her and the other two men jammed in the doorway. No time to laugh. No way to take hostages, either, because it might be days before Snake rode in.

"Let them go!" he shouted and headed for the fireplace.

Foster was unconscious, bleeding to death very messily—an incredible river of blood. Stalwart could feel sorry for him, because he had probably been tricked into being enslaved, and after that he would have had no choice.

He was not sorry for Thrusk, who had been just as bad before Skuldigger bespelled him. Incredibly, the giant had managed to sit up. He was hardly bleeding at all, just blowing red froth out from under his beard, gurgling and coughing blood. Stalwart went around him and took up the branding iron, resisting a powerful temptation to let Thrusk have a taste of it. He poked it into the roof instead.

Thrusk reached feebly for his fallen sword.

Stalwart kicked it out of reach. "I told you," he said. "You're dying! Outsmarted by a kid. I'm glad." The antique thatch flared up. "Can't stay to watch, but take all the time you want."

Emerald was staring at Stalwart as if he'd sprouted antlers. "You really are a Blade! That was what I was detecting—all those years of training!"

"If you say so. Come on." He pointed at Foster's sword. "Bring that."

He ran to the door and hurled the iron onto the roof of the next shack. The sea breeze was still blowing, and all the village thatch was old and dry. A good blaze or two would distract the pursuit. People were shouting in the distance, but no one had come in sight yet. The moon was

... *there* ... and just short of the full, so that was east. When they brought him in through the gate the sun had just set on his left so the river must be over ... *there*. "This way!"

He stretched out his left hand behind him. "Hang on and don't trip me with that sword, but keep it. You may need it." It was dark in the alleyways and the footing was made treacherous by garbage, firewood, wheelbarrows, chicken coops—all sorts of clutter. He went as fast as he dared, feeling out the clearance with his sword and judging direction by the moonlight on the clouds.

"Wart, there are monsters out there!"

"There are worse monsters in here."

He ducked under windows and turned away from candlelight spilling from doorways. He collided with a hurdle across his path and wakened a litter of piglets on the other side of it to terrified squealing. He kept heading west.

"There are two Sisters and a child, Wart! We can't leave them."

Oh, death and flames! "We must leave them! They'll be safer here for a few more days than they will be out in the woods with us." His job was to rescue Emerald and lead Snake to the traitors' lair, in that order.

The shouting in the background was increasing, and sometimes when he looked back he could see two red pillars of sparks. Glowing fragments were floating away in the breeze,

threatening half the village. With any luck Skuldigger and his cronies would concentrate their
own efforts on putting out the fire and rely on
the chimeras to catch the fugitives for them.
With a lot more luck they would be wrong.

The unbroken wall on his right must be the
palisade. "The gate's that way," he whispered,
"but they'll be watching it. We need a place to
climb over."

"Why not just push it down? It's rotten."

He tried a shoulder against it. "I'm not stalwart enough." The individual posts might be no
thicker than a man's arm, but they were still
sturdy hunks of timber.

"Keep trying. There are places where it's
mush."

Emerald had seen it in daylight and probably
seen more of it than he had. Together they crept
along the perimeter of the village, hunting for a
weak point, often having to detour around
heaps of garbage. Unfortunately none of the ob-
stacles was high enough to let them climb over
the wall. As he began to worry that they were
drawing too close to the gate and its inevitable
guards, he almost collided with a pole angled
across his path. Fumbling and peering, he made
out that there were four of them, and they were
bracing up a section of the palisade that was
anxious to fall inward.

He handed his sword to Emerald and set to
work. The props came loose easily enough. Then

the wall sagged farther, but its cross-rails still held it together. He was certain his time was running out fast. He took up one of the props and tried to find a place he could insert it to use as a pry bar.

"Wart!"

"What?"

"There's something out there!" Emerald's voice was shrill.

"Good." *Got it!*—he forced the lever between two posts. "Need all the help we can get."

"Wart! I am telling you! There is a chimera outside that fence. And at least one more not far away."

"Help me!" He heaved with all his strength.

Emerald, having her hands full of swords, put her shoulder to the pole. Timber groaned, and then a single post cracked off and toppled, bringing two lengths of cross-rail with it. Not enough. He was about to put his lever back and try again when a wailing animal howl froze him solid. It went on and on until his scalp prickled. The lungs on that thing! Whatever was creating that racket was not close, but it must be big— *very* big.

Something grunted just outside the narrow gap he had made. He dropped the pole and grabbed his sword back. Another post creaked, snapped, and fell. No need to break out now. The thing outside was breaking in.

Fright

It WAS UNFORTUNATE THAT THE MOON CHOSE that moment to wander into a cloud, so that Stalwart and Emerald, watching from behind a chicken coop some distance away, were unable to make out many details of what happened. Or perhaps that was fortunate. Whatever the new-comer looked like, it roared and growled, it made the entire stockade shake, it broke off posts and threw them away like straws. And finally it lurched in through the gap it had created and paused to sniff and snuffle. It was about the size of a bull and seemed uncertain whether it should stand on two legs or four. Its bushy tail was as large as a feather bed. Eventually it decided to go straight ahead and lumbered off between two huts.

Stalwart wiped his forehead. He managed to swallow at his third attempt. The weapon of choice against a thing like that would be a lance with warhorse and full plate mail included. "I am inclined to get out of here."

"Wait for the next one," Emerald whispered. They were kneeling very close together and he could feel her shaking. He had an arm around her, was why. She had one around him and they could shake in unison. "It's coming."

"You're sure? The fire must have drawn them." He could hear it. The sky was red over the center of the village.

"Possibly, but also they've eaten the fens bare. They either have to go after farmers' livestock or come back here. They're spelled to stay away, but hunger—"

"Sh!" Something was snuffling outside the stockade. The moonlight was brightening rapidly.

A couple of houses away someone screamed terribly—the newcomer had made its presence known. Then the second chimera entered. It leaped through the gap and ran after the first one so quickly that Stalwart wasn't *quite* sure what he'd seen. It was bigger than the first. A rat with arms walking on its hind legs would about sum it up. Tusks? Well, he wasn't sure about the tusks. Its tread had made the ground tremble.

"Let's go," he said, finding his throat drier than ever. "Outside is the lesser of two evils."

"I wish I knew that," Emerald said, but she

was with him as he scrambled through the gap in the stockade. "You're not going to go right out in the woods, are you?"

"I'm going back to report to Snake. I'm going to hand you over to him and tell him I've brought you back safe and sound, so I've carried out my mission and please can I go off and do something much safer for the next ten years, like guarding the King from attacks by lion-size dogs. . . ." He followed the stockade around, through a young growth of saplings and spindly weeds, hoping he might find an unguarded boat on the river. "And he can take his Old Blades and turn them into sausages for all I care."

"Wart! You'll—I'm sorry! I should be calling you 'Sir Stalwart.' "

"My friends still call me Wart." *And my enemies die!* "And you're going to be Sister Emerald again—if you still want to be."

"Ha! I shall tell Mother Superior she can stuff her precious Sisters and use them for garden furniture."

He chuckled and said, "Sh!" There were voices ahead. He crept forward as quietly as he could. All dry twigs near the settlement had long since been gathered up for kindling, but total silence was still impossible.

"There's more chimeras around," Emerald whispered.

"Which way?"

"Hmm . . . All around."

He reached the corner of the stockade and knelt to peer along the waterfront. With the tide out a silvery trickle in the center of the channel was all that remained of the river. The rest was black mud. There could be no thought of boating home.

The voices he had heard came from a gang of men gathering water to fight the fire. They were too few to form a proper chain. The one on the end filled a bucket and trudged over to meet the next, who gave him an empty one in exchange, then walked the full one to the next man, and so on. They were all quite visible in the moonlight and the glow of the fire. Their cause seemed hopeless. Probably they were trying to wet down the other roofs and the village wells couldn't keep up with demand.

"I'm going to take my shoes off," Stalwart whispered. "That mud'll suck 'em off if I don't. It'll be horrible going but still easier than trying to force a way through the brush." They would have moonlight; the woods were dark.

"Wart, Wart! That is crazy! We'll wander for days and days and go around in circles."

"You do that if you want," he said, pulling off his left shoe. "I'm going back the way we came." Right shoe. "Didn't you take note?"

"I got dizzy in the first few minutes." Emerald was removing her shoes too. Perhaps girls just enjoyed arguing. There were no girls at Ironhall, but there would be lots of them at court.

"When we embarked we went to the left and the village was on the left bank. We passed six channels on the right and only two on the left. So we go right, stay on this bank, cross channels twice, and then look for our tracks. If we can't find those, we'll cut inland at dawn. Ready?"

She stood up, holding her shoes. "You think you're pretty smart, don't you?"

"Oh yes. Also brave, handsome, witty, charming, trustworthy, and modest. Now let's—"

Two chimeras burst out of the trees on the far bank and flashed across the empty channel. The bucket gang fled, screaming, but one of them was run down. A chimera knocked him flat, and—as far as Stalwart could make out at that distance—bit through his spinal cord with its beak. Then it picked him up in its arms and walked back the way it had come. The second chimera seemed to have two heads. It loped on all fours into Quagmarsh and the gate remained open and unguarded behind it.

"Cloud!" Emerald said. "And Swan and her baby!"

"They'll be all right. They can tell where the chimeras are, can't they, just like you can? Besides, Skuldigger values them, so he'll see they're protected. Now let's go."

The mud made for horrible walking, every step sinking ankle deep into frigid muck full of rotten branches and old shells. But it was better than fighting through bushes, and there was room to see danger approaching—anything Emerald's sensitivity missed. There was room to swing a sword.

The night was alive. Owls still hunted; the bat population was intact, with its creepy whistling cries. Chimeras were howling all over the fens, but Stalwart had no way of knowing whether they were calling to one another or just expressing rage and hunger. The fire's glow remained visible behind them for a long time.

Emerald held her sword in her left hand and clung to him with her right, which he found quite flattering. He could even admit it was comforting under the circumstance, although poor tactics. It certainly was not a romantic moment. Their feet went *squoosh—squoosh—squoosh* . . . and monsters howled, *arrrgh—arrrgh—*

She began turning her head a lot, searching. . . .

"Trouble?" he murmured.

"Close." After a few more steps she muttered, "Very close." Then she stopped. "Wart, we're heading for a chimera. It's just up ahead a little, waiting for us."

He had that swallowing problem again. "Then it knows we're here. Let's keep going. We should just show it that we're not afraid of it."

"You show it. I'm scared to death."

"So am I, but the chimera doesn't know that."

Her nails dug into his arm. "Wart! There!" She transferred her sword to her right hand.

It took him a moment to see what she had made out in the tricky silver moonlight. Something huge and dark stood within the trees, watching them. If Thrusk had been a five-year-old, that is what he would have looked like when he grew up. Except its eyes were too far apart. It had a muzzle . . . and horns. It was furry. He couldn't hope to win against that thing—chimeras were just too fast, too strong, and probably much too loathe to die. Obviously the thing Dreadnought had killed had been a chimera, but he had been one of three Blades at the start of the fight. The other two hadn't won any jeweled stars to wear on their jerkins.

This was what real fear felt like. Hard to breathe.

Seeing that it had been noticed, the monster displayed a mouthful of fangs like an ivory chess set, and growled a low, rumbling, deathly sound.

"Speak to it!" Emerald said.

"*Speak* to it?"

"Poor wretch! He must have some human intelligence still lurking inside there. He should be at least as smart as a dog."

Well, it was worth a try. Stalwart strained his throat to sound deep and commanding. "Go home!" He pointed back to the village. "Food there! Go home. Go to the Doctor. Doctor Skuldigger. He has food for you. Go home!" He added under his breath, "Eat him, for all I care . . . Bad Boy."

The chimera turned its head to look where he had pointed.

"Go home!" Stalwart repeated. He went through the message again.

The monster threw back its head and uttered a great, long, pitiable howl that raised the hair on his neck. Then it vanished, without sound or any sense of motion. It just was not there any more.

It could probably return the same way.

"Come along, Sister." Stalwart resumed the trek. "You will," he said—and for some reason he was whispering—"tell me if it changes its mind and comes after us?" She probably wouldn't have time to get two words out.

"I'll try to remember."

"Let me get him at first and *poke* with that sword. Don't swing it or you're liable to get me instead."

But nothing more happened. They walked on unmolested. He had not died of fright—Stalwart, *Sir* Stalwart. He was going to be a hero if his luck would just hold a little longer. But then . . .

They were approaching a fork in the mud highway. Hmm! If the punt had brought him along the branch presently to his left, then the branch to his right must be one of the two he had seen joining from his (then) left, so he and Emerald should now cross and go down the other. But if the punt had come along the one now to his right, then the one to his (now) left must be one of the several he had seen joining from his (then) right and should be ignored. All the channels looked the same by moonlight. His wonderful clever plan had just collapsed and all his bragging to Emerald had been vanity and wind. The safest thing to do was to stay on the right bank and keep walking. If Quagmarsh was on an island they would eventually come back to it, although they might reach the sea first. And the best that could happen would be the two channels he had seen on his left earlier turning out to be the same channel, a loop around an island, and in that case this new plan would get them where they wanted to be anyway, although they probably wouldn't recognize the spot in the dark.

Trusting him, Emerald did not comment as they went past the fork, bearing right. Instead she said, "Was the archlute your idea?"

"No, that was Snake's. I wondered if I'd ever be able to bring myself to smash a beautiful thing like that. You know, it wasn't difficult at all?"

"You said you added some ideas."

"Just one, I think. The rusty old sword. They wanted me to be unarmed, saying I would be less likely to get my throat cut if I seemed harmless. I argued that carters always carry some sort of a weapon, so I would seem unusual if I didn't. I settled for a really absurd old relic that Vincent found in a stable."

"And you very nearly got both of us filled full of crossbow bolts!"

He laughed, although he knew he had not been laughing at the time. "No I didn't! They weren't going to shoot with Skuldigger's coach right behind us; not to mention the Doctor himself and all those splendid horses."

"That fall you took off the wagon . . . ?"

"Cute, wasn't it? I told you I learned some tumbling and juggling and stuff when I was with Owain, and I kept it up at Ironhall. Even taught some of the others. It helps keep you supple."

"You were faking?"

"Of course. Owain taught me some sleight of hand—pulling coins out of kids' ears and so on. The secret to that sort of trick is that you set it up beforehand and you distract the viewers at the critical moment. That was what I was doing. I played the fool with the sword so I would be written off as a fool." His jaw still throbbed. "I didn't expect Thrusk to take it quite so seriously."

They squelched on for a while, and then Emerald said, "You're very brave."

He thought about it. "I'd like to believe that, but I wouldn't do it again. Crazy, more than brave. I've learned a lot these last two days. . . . Besides, you should talk—you've been marvelous!"

"I," Emerald said grimly, "was given no choice."

"I didn't have much," he admitted. Bandit and then Snake had flattered him into it. He would never fall for that trick again!

They came to another fork and again he kept to the right. The night was lasting forever. His feet hurt, every muscle in his legs ached, and he wasn't going to suggest stopping before she did.

"At least we seem to be past all the chimeras," he said. "I don't hear any howling ahead of us, do you?"

"I hear something."

Oh! So did he.

After a moment she said, "What *is* that?" And after another, "Oh, Wart! There must be hundreds of them! They're coming this way, Wart!"

He stopped. Suddenly reaction set in and he felt so limp he wondered how he was managing to stay upright. Maybe it was the mud holding him up. "The garlic was Vincent's idea."

"*Wart!?*" she cried. "What do you mean?"

"You don't have such a thing as a dog biscuit on you, do you?"

"Dogs? Those are dogs coming?"

"Garlic doesn't smell all that strong if you keep it in cloves, or bulbs," he said wearily. "It's when you cut it up it stinks. Nobody wanting to transport garlic would ever dream of grinding it up and mixing it with salt first."

"Oh!" she said. "The barrels leaked? Gaps between the planks in the wagon and the road was very bumpy? You left a trail of garlic!"

"Dogs love garlic. Absolutely crazy about it. And we didn't plan this part, but I fell in the stuff when the wagon broke down. Then Thrusk made me run the rest of the way to the river. It wasn't much fun while it lasted, but if he'd put me on a horse, the dogs might have lost the trail."

The dogs were clearly audible now, Snake and his men coming at last. If old Sir Vincent was with them, as he probably was, he would have remembered the abandoned hamlet of Quagmarsh and guessed that was where the conspirators were holed up. Not having boats, the Old Blades would have had to wait for the tide to go out. It occurred to Sir Stalwart that he had left very little for them to do.

Valglorious

From the outside Valglorious looked like a castle, and it had withstood sieges in the past. Inside, it was a ducal palace. After two days of luxury, Emerald began to feel spoiled for any lesser existence. She had been assigned a bedchamber the size of a ballroom, she had maids to attend her, she chose her clothes from a finer wardrobe than she had ever imagined, and the entire resources of the palace were available to amuse her. She seriously considered writing herself a note, *Memo: Marry a duke*.

From Wart's stories she had expected her host to be big, but Sir Vincent was sturdy and short, wearing his years well. He was also brusque, charming, considerate, and took no nonsense from anyone. His wife, whom Wart had not mentioned at all, was everybody's idea of what a grandmother ought to be. She could not have been kinder.

On the third morning Emerald went riding

with Wart, who looked much better since he'd been healed at the elementary in Kysbury but was still steamingly furious at having been kept out of the fighting at Quagmarsh. When they returned, they were informed that Sir Vincent wished to see them. They found him standing in his favorite place, before the fireplace in the great hall. He was chatting to another man, who was exceedingly lean, with a supercilious manner and a thin mustache to match. Emerald had met him only once and then briefly, by moonlight in a swamp. He was clean and neatly dressed, but his eyes looked as if they had been propped open for a week. He bowed very low to her.

"You are in good health, I trust, Sister?"

She gave him a bob in return. "Recovering, Sir Snake." No thanks to him! "And I am not a Sister." Thanks to him!

"Yes, you are. The annals of the Companionship record nothing to the contrary."

She would see about that. "Cloud? Swan?"

"Both safe!" Snake beamed triumphantly. "Sister Cloud is upstairs being bathed and scented and pampered and whatever else ladies' maids do to ladies. Sister Swan and her daughter have been joyously reunited with their family." He pouted briefly in Wart's direction. "Skuldigger and a few others eluded us, I am afraid. But we caught enough of the ringleaders to stage an impressive public execution." And to Emerald, "With all the usual barbarities imposed on traitors. Let me know if you want tickets."

"I'll think about it."

"You may be called to give evidence at the trial. Ten minutes ought to do it."

"Casualties?" asked Sir Vincent.

"A few. Not too bad," Snake said evasively. He turned his bleary, red-rimmed eyes back to Wart. "Fetch your lute and anything else you need, brother. We ride for Grandon at once."

"Yes, brother!" Wart turned and ran. He hurtled up the staircase in a tattoo of boots on timber.

The Blades exchanged amused glances that Emerald found excessively irritating. Wart was a *hero* and they were still thinking of him a child. It was his courage that had made this victory possible.

"You have a visitor, Sister," said Sir Vincent. "Mother Superior is waiting upstairs in the solarium."

Oh! She had been expecting a summons to Oakendown. Having the queen bee come to her was probably an epochal honor and breach of tradition. "Let her wait."

Snake pursed his lips disapprovingly. "Is that a sensible attitude under the circumstances?"

"I may drop in later and spit in her eye."

He sank down gracefully, kneeling to her. "If there is eye spitting to be done, mistress, then I am the guilty party. Which eye do you want—right or left?''

She did not look at Sir Vincent, but she knew he was amused. "You were merely doing your duty. Mother Superior betrayed my trust!''

Snake shrugged and rose, still moving with a fencer's grace. "As she will freely admit, although the King did threaten to clap her in irons. I am quite sure she will kneel to you and beg your forgiveness. What else do you want? Now is the time to ask.''

"Gentleholme Sanctuary!'' she said. "My father—''

"Already done!'' Snake smiled his infuriatingly condescending smile again. "We received more complaints about Gentleholme than almost any other elementary in all Chivial. It was one of the first we raided, back in Thirdmoon. A couple of the rogues turned king's evidence and the rest were hanged.''

"So they did murder my father?''

"We cannot be certain in specific cases.'' He shrugged. He was waiting for her to say something. . . .

"And what of the money they stole from him, then?'' she asked. "What of the land?'' What of her mother, aging in poverty these past four years?

He sighed. "There have been thousands of such cases over the years, Sister. To locate and compensate the victims would be an impossible task. Under the law, all assets are forfeit to the Crown."

"How nice for His Majesty! Perhaps Doctor Skuldigger does have a valid point or two!"

Sir Vincent cleared his throat warningly. "May I suggest, Sister? Sir Snake, Mother Superior, and of course the King—they are all persons of power and authority. Such people frequently have to stray outside the normal bounds of conscience in performing their duties. What I mean is that you will not get very far by trying to shame any of them into admitting guilt. You certainly will gain nothing by spitting in eyes."

"But . . . ?" she said cautiously, wondering if the old man was trying to be helpful or was in league with his fellow Blade.

"But if this story should come out, then Mother Superior would certainly have to resign her high office. The King would be forced to dismiss Sir Snake, possibly commit him to trial. Ambrose himself would look like a coward who had sent a girl into terrible danger just to save his own skin."

Snake shuddered dramatically but said nothing.

"Do continue, Sir Vincent. Your discourse is most interesting," she said.

Vincent shrugged. "Now, while you have Mother Superior on her knees, you could ask for immediate restitution as Sister, a solemn prom-

ise of promotion to Mother within a year, a posting to court, if that is your wish—just about
anything that takes your fancy. As for our sov-
ereign lord the King, if he has fallen heir to
lands stolen from your family, you might offer
to take them off his hands as compensation for
your suffering." He smiled then. "You would
have to promise to keep your mouth shut, of
course—not about Stalwart's valor but about
how you were deliberately exposed to danger.
That must never be revealed."

She looked at Snake, whose face would have
seemed as innocent as a baby's had babies
sported supercilious mustaches. "Would the
King give up Peachyard?"

"Give up Peachyard?" he echoed incredu-
lously. "And I suppose you would also expect
all appurtenances pertaining thereto, including
but not limited to all livestock, standing crops,
indentured laborers, vehicles, implements, existing buildings, and improvements? You might
even demand a five-year relief from taxes and a
cash grant of, say, ten thousand crowns for necessary repairs?"

It would not bring back her father, nor yet her
brothers, but it would be fun breaking this news
to her mother. . . . She blinked away some tears.
She nodded. "Not a penny less."

"No spreading naughty stories?"

"My lips are sealed."

"No spitting on Mother Superior?"

"I may drool a bit, but no more than that."

Snake took her fingers and kissed them. "Consider it done, mistress. You were most helpful."

Wart came down the grand staircase like a landslide and seemed to bounce across the floor until he came to a panting stop beside Sir Snake. "Ready!" He had his lute on his back.

"Then we must be on our way," Snake said. He offered a hand to Vincent. "Thank you for all your help, brother. Where is your dear lady? Anything we can do for you in return?"

"You can tell Fat Man to keep that spotty duke out of my hair for another year or ten."

"I'll see if I can get him kidnapped."

"Preferably by Baels."

Emerald held out both hands to Wart. "Thanks for saving me from the monsters, even if you did throw me to them in the first place. I'm truly grateful. Good chance, Sir Stalwart! See you at court."

He blinked and then grinned. "So you will!"

Star

WHATEVER ONE MIGHT THINK OF SNAKE AS taskmaster, the man never spared himself either. It was almost midnight when he and Stalwart thundered into the King's favorite palace of Nocare, west of Grandon. He had not had a proper night's sleep in a week, but he saw Stalwart temporarily quartered in the guest wing, ordered a tailor dragged out of bed to measure him, and then went off in his road-stained clothes to report to the Lord Chancellor.

Soon after dawn the tailor got his revenge by dragging Stalwart out of bed to try on his Guard livery, all blue and silver. It was much too loose on him, so the man fussed angrily with chalk and a mouthful of pins, marking it for alteration. Probably it was the smallest uniform ever cut and he had not been able to believe his own measurements. During this ordeal, surveying himself in the mirror, Stalwart was more depressed than impressed. He *felt* a great deal older than he had done when he left Ironhall two weeks ago, but he didn't *look* it. His moorland haircut helped not at all. Those ears of his were definitely better kept out of sight. He had Sleight hanging at his thigh, a magnificent rapier with a cat's eye pommel, and he looked ... *ridiculous!*

This way to the children's pageant.

Snake walked in without knocking. He beamed, fresh as dew on a mushroom. "Good chance, brother! Oh, very smart! How is it?"

"A few minor adjustments," the tailor mumbled around the pins.

"Don't take too long. He's going to be presented at noon."

The tailor practically screamed. He ripped the livery off Stalwart and vanished out the door with it, leaving scissors and tape and other tools strewn everywhere. Stalwart looked around for other clothes. There weren't any, because his riding outfit had gone to be washed. He perched on the edge of the bed in his briefs and regarded Snake's contented smile with considerable suspicion.

Snake leaned against the wall and looked as guiltless as paint. He was wearing full court dress, with pearls and gold trim and his White Star order. "While I remember", he said, "you will sup with His Majesty this evening. Bring your lute. Private party, with music. I advise you to stay sober and not to eat too much at the state banquet this afternoon."

"I always sick up at state banquets," Stalwart said sourly.

"I look forward to that, then. At noon the Fat Man will be *holding court*. A very big event—heralds and trumpets and the best gravy. It will begin with the new ambassador from Isilond presenting his credentials. Then the Lord Chancellor—that's Durendal now, of course—will present me."

"*You?* Does the K—does Fat Man have such a short memory?"

"Two more points," Snake said smugly, flicking the four-pointed star on his breast. He meant he had been promoted from member to officer.

"Wonderful!" Stalwart said. It was a rare honor for any Blade, very rare. He jumped up and pumped Snake's hand and tried to look and sound excited. "Well earned, too!" No need to say *who* had done the earning.

"Thank you, brother. It's an acknowledgment of all the Old Blades' efforts, of course." Snake did not believe that, obviously, but he must enjoy saying it that way so you knew he didn't believe it. "You'll go next. This is a breach of precedent and tradition, so we had to make it up. We gave you extra trumpets. Leader will present you. When he announces you—Bandit, I mean, not the herald—then you advance doing the three bows thing. You kneel on the cushion—"

"*I do what?*" Stalwart yelled, leaping up from the bed again.

"Kneel on the cushion," Snake repeated, as if surprised by his surprise. "His Majesty will place the ribbon over your head and—"

"What *ribbon?*"

"Member of the White Star, of course." A grin broke through, and now it was Snake's turn to pump hands. "Congratulations! The King's own idea, not mine. He is *really* impressed by what you did, brother. You are only the seventh Blade ever admitted to the Star. The heralds think you must be the youngest member ever, by about ten years."

Stalwart muttered, "Flames!" a few times and flopped down on the bed again. If he'd been earning *that* then he must have been in much worse danger than he'd realized. How low had they rated his chances? He shivered all over.

"You deserve it, brother."

"That's what I'm afraid of." But had he earned it? Or was he being given a diamond-studded bauble so that he wouldn't provoke too many smirks when he strutted around the palace dressed up as a Blade?

"The bad news," Snake added, "is that Fat Man says he may just create a junior order of chivalry especially for you and Sister Emerald— the Order of the King's Daggers."

"Oh, funny! Very, *very* funny!"

"It's funny when he says it, brother! Kings' jokes are always hilarious. If he says it again tonight, you laugh your head off!"

"I don't, he'll chop it off?"

"Could be," Snake agreed with a smirk. "Now this afternoon . . . at these highfalutin formal affairs, it is customary to have four Blades in attendance on the dais. Leader has assigned today's duty to Sir Orvil, Sir Panther, Sir Dragon, and Sir Rufus."

"*Flames!*" Stalwart was saying that a lot this morning. Those four, who thought he had been chucked out or had run off with his tail between his legs, were going to watch him being inducted into the Star? Bandit would be there, and the great Durendal. Flames, flames, flames! Life was *never* going to get sweeter than this.

Snake wandered over to the window and peered out. "That's if you want it that way," he said offhandedly.

Warning gongs clanged. "What other way might I want it?" Stalwart asked warily.

Snake shrugged. Even in formal court finery he was skinny. "We haven't nabbed Skuldigger yet or his wife. We think Baron Grimshank is worth a hard look. And there are many, many others out there almost as bad."

"Oh, no! *No!* You are not going to talk me into any more of your crazy suicide missions!"

"Of course not," Snake said blandly to the

window pane. "You'll enjoy hanging around here with a hundred other men, all guarding the King. Standing on the sidelines at balls, masques, banquets . . . You'll love it, I'm sure. Ten years of crushing boredom to look forward to. I admit it isn't as boring as it used to be, but it's we Old Blades who are really doing the work—the cutting edge you might say. Out there in the real world battling evil, defeating the King's enemies—"

"I am not an Old Blade! I am the youngest Blade of them all, perhaps the youngest ever bound. . . . When am I going to be bound?"

"When Ambrose gets around to it. Next time he goes to Ironhall. Of course you can't wear a sword in his presence until you are bound. Neither can I these days, but I don't care, because I'm not in the Royal Guard. That *will* be embarrassing, an unarmed Blade! Goodness! Still, I'm sure you can find lots of other boys in the palace to play with."

"Burn you!" Stalwart muttered.

"Meanwhile I need a man who can handle a really tricky mission. He has to be the sort who won't attract suspicion, who can think on his feet, a superlative—"

"No! No, no, no! You are trying to sucker me into volunteering again! You and the King! You are going to cheat me out of my reward!"

Snake turned, looking indignant. "Not at all! Just a brief postponement. We'd keep you under wraps for a week or two longer, that's all. The Star is yours, only you would receive it at that private supper tonight instead of in public. We'd put the livery away in a drawer for now. That's all." He picked up the tailor's shears and tested their edge with his thumb.

There was a long silence.

"Of course, you did swear an oath . . . but if you're not interested you're not interested." He turned back to the window.

Still silence.

Snake sighed. "It is so hard to find really first-rate men! Superlative fencers, I mean—great swordsmen who are also men of courage. Above all, courage. Tremendous courage. You're the only man I know who could possibly have achieved what I had in mind."

Oh, flames!

"What do you want me to do this time?" Stalwart asked glumly.

Young Sir Stalwart's story begins with "Book One of the King's Daggers," but the world of the legendary order of knights is first introduced in
The Gilded Chain:
A Tale of the King's Blades
by Dave Duncan,
now available from Avon Eos.

As unwanted, rebellious boys, they found refuge in the grim school of Ironhall. They emerged years later as nimble and deadly young men, the finest in the realm—the King's Blades. A magical ritual of a sword through the heart bound each of them to absolute loyalty to defend his ward—if not the King himself—then whomever else he designated. And the greatest Blade of them all was Sir Durendal.

But a lifelong dream of riding to war at the side of his adored liege—of battling traitors and monsters and rising high in the court—is dashed when Durendal is bonded till death, not to his beloved King, but an effete noble fop. Yet from this inauspicious beginning, twisting destiny has many strange and inscrutable plans for the young knight, prophesied to be the mightiest hero that ever lived.

SOMEHOW LOVE POINT SEEMED INAPPROPRIATE for the still-sniveling Marquis, but he was back there. Now Durendal stood opposite, at death. He was flanked by Byless and Gotherton. He wondered if they would be strong enough to restrain him when his reflexes took over, and if a man could cut himself to shreds from the inside out. The singing was over. The Brat had trilled the dedication, wheyfaced and staring at Prime with owlish eyes, as he laid another sword on the anvil.

Master of Rituals had invoked the spirits, and either he had summoned far more than before or else Durendal was just more attuned to them. He sensed the haunted chamber quivering with power. Spirituality fizzed in his blood. Strange lights dancing over the stonework made every shadow numinous. His hand itched to take up the superb weapon gleaming on the anvil.

The Marquis had shrunk till he looked like a

shivering, cowed child compared to the awesome Grand Master. Could a real man serve such a craven nothing all his life without going crazy? Could Durendal endure to be only an ornament, as poor Harvest had put it? Yes, by the spirits! This was what he had aimed for, worked for, struggled for—to be one of the King's Blades. If his ward was useless in himself, then he would still have the finest protector in all Chivial. Perhaps a man might make something out of that worthless human rag if he tried hard enough, or perhaps the King had some secret, dangerous mission in mind for him. With real luck, there would be a war, when a young noble would be expected to raise a regiment and his Blade could go into battle at his side.

The invocation ended. At last it was his move, his moment, his triumph—five years he had worked for this! He turned to summon Gotherton forward, felt Gotherton's fingers shake as he unbuttoned the shirt. He winked and almost laughed aloud at the disbelief he saw flood over the boyish face. In that oppressive heat, it was a relief to shed the garment, to flex his shoulders, and spin around. He winked at Byless also when he came, and this time was rewarded with a stare of open admiration. Why were they all so worried? Things only went wrong once every hundred years or so. He was not poor Harvest! He was the second Durendal, come into his destiny. He felt the thumb press on his chest, the cool touch of charcoal.

Now for that sword! *His* sword. Oh, bliss! It floated in his hand. Blue starlight gleamed and danced along the blade and a bar of gold fire burned in the cat's eye cabochon on the pommel. He wanted to whirl it, caress it with a strop until it would cut falling gossamer, hold it in sunlight and admire the damask—but those luxuries must wait. He sprang up onto the anvil.

"My lord Marquis of Nutting!" The echoes rumbled and rolled—wonderful! "Upon my soul, I, Durendal, candidate in the Loyal and Ancient Order of the King's Blades, do irrevocably swear in the presence of these my brethren that I will evermore defend you against all foes, setting my own life as nothing to shield you from peril, reserving only my fealty to our lord the King. To bind me to this oath, I bid you plunge this my sword into my heart that I may die if I swear falsely or, being true, may live by the power of the spirits here assembled to serve you until in time I die again."

Then down to the floor and down on one knee.

Sallow and trembling, the Marquis accepted the sword, seeming ready to drop it at any moment. Durendal rose and stepped back until he felt the anvil against his calves. He sat.

Grand Master pulled the Marquis forward. He needed both hands to raise the sword this time.

It wavered, flashing firelight, and the point made uncertain circles around the target—idiot! It would do no good if it missed Durendal's heart, no good at all. He waited until the terrified noble looked up enough to meet his eyes. Then he smiled encouragingly and raised his arms. Byless and Gotherton pulled them back, bracing them against their waists. He must try not to thrash too hard when the shock came. He waited. He could hear Nutting's teeth chatter.

"Do it now!" he said. He was about to add, "Do it right!" but the Marquis shrieked, "Serve or die!" and thrust the sword. Either he remembered Durendal's instructions or he lost his footing, for he stumbled forward and the steel razored instantly through muscle, ribs, heart, lung, more ribs, and out into the space beyond. The guard thudded against Durendal's chest.

It did hurt. He had expected pain at the wound, but his whole body exploded with it. Through that furnace of agony he became aware of two terrified eyes staring into his. He wanted to say, "You must take it out again quickly, my lord," but speaking with a sword through his chest proved difficult.

Grand Master hauled Nutting back bodily. Fortunately he remembered to take the sword with him.

Durendal looked down to watch the wound heal. The trickle of blood was astonishingly small, but then it always was—a heart could not pump when it had a nail through it. He felt the healing, a tickling sensation right through to his back, and also a huge surge of power and excitement and pride. Byless and Gotherton had released him. The Forge thundered with cheers, which seemed like an unnecessary commotion, although he'd always cheered for others in the past. A binding was routine, nothing to it.

He was a Blade, a companion in the Order. People would address him as Sir Durendal, although that was only a courtesy title.

"You didn't need us!" Gotherton gasped. "You barely twitched!"

They could be thanked later, and the Brat, the armorers, and all the others. First things first. He rose and went to recover his sword before the glazed-looking Marquis dropped her. Now he could inspect her properly. She was a hand-and-a-half sword with a straight blade, about a yard long, the longest he could wear at his belt without tripping. She was single-edged for two-thirds of her length, double-edged near the point. He admired the grace of the fluted quillons, the delicate sweep of the knuckle guard, the finger ring for when he wanted to use her as a rapier, the fire of the cat's-eye pommel that gave her her balance, which of course was perfect, neither too far forward for thrusting nor so far back that he would not be able to slash. The armorers had created a perfect all-around weapon for a swordsman of unusual versatility.

Had they laid her among a hundred others, he would have picked her out as his. He admired his own heart's blood on her, then slipped her through the loop on his belt. He would name her Harvest—a good name for a sword, a tribute to a friend who'd been treated badly by chance.

Byless was fussing, trying to help him into his shirt, Grand Master was congratulating him, while he was still trying to think of all the people he must thank before . . .

Suddenly his attention was caught by the Marquis, that green-faced, shivering pimp in the background. How strange! It was as if that pseudo-aristocratic ninny was the only illuminated thing in the room, with everyone and everything else in darkness. Nobody, nothing else mattered. The turd was still a turd, unfortunately—the binding had not changed that—but now he was obviously an important turd. He must be looked after and kept safe.

Most-wondrous!

Sir Durendal walked over to his ward and nodded respectfully.

"At your service now, my lord," he said. "When do we ride?"

DAVE DUNCAN is an award-winning author whose fantasy trilogy, *The Seventh Sword*, is considered a sword-and-sorcery classic. His numerous novels include *Lord of the Fire Lands*, *The Gilded Chain*, *Strings*, *Hero*, the popular tetrologies, *A Man of his Word* and *A Handful of Men*, and the remarkable, critically acclaimed fantasy trilogy, *The Great Game*.

AVON EOS PRESENTS
MASTERS OF FANTASY AND ADVENTURE

A SECRET HISTORY
The Book of Ash #1
by Mary Gentle   78869-1/$6.99 US

THE GILDED CHAIN:
A Tale of the King's Blades
by Dave Duncan   79126-9/$6.99 US/$8.99 CAN

THE DAUGHTERS OF BAST: THE HIDDEN LAND
by Sarah Isidore   80318-6/$6.50 US/$8.50 CAN

SCENT OF MAGIC
by Andre Norton   78416-5/$6.50 US/$8.50 CAN

THE DEATH OF THE NECROMANCER
by Martha Wells   78814-4/$6.99 US/$8.99 CAN